NIPPING THEM IN THE BUD

EDWARD LEE

deadite press

DEADITE PRESS
833 SE Main Street #342
Portland, OR 97214
www.DEADITEPRESS.com

An imprint of Eraserhead Press
www.eraserheadpress.com

ISBN: 978-1-62105-111-4

ACKNOWLEDGMENTS

Christine Morgan, Rose O'Keefe, John Baltisberger, K. Trap Jones, Dave Wilson, Roman, Gary Hguonodcm, Hector Fonseca, Brandon Thompson, Craig M. Steele, Peggy Howes, Gordon Jones, Dustin LaValley, Daniel Volpe, Tommy865, Chris Newton, Artur Kouri, Voracious Gnome, John Petitt, James Flynn, Phobophile, The Book Dweller, somegorilla, Lydia Peever, Jessica Hause.

NIPPING THEM IN THE BUD

Sharsted rarely remembered his dreams, and when he did they were almost never nightmares. But *this? This is definitely a nightmare,* he thought. What did it look like? He couldn't *see* anything, for everything that extended before his vision was the blackest of pitch-black. He might as well have been locked up in a shipping container and fully buried a hundred feet deep. Not so much as a pin-prick speck of light infiltrated his confines.

And just what *were* his confines? There was no telling up front—of course not; he couldn't see anything. He could feel his own body in the blackness, though: arms, chest, legs, etc. He could feel that his legs were extended, but there was no impression that he was standing on anything, like, say, a floor.

Was he floating, then? Like someone in a sensory deprivation tank? Well, no, because he *could* sense some things; not just touch, but hearing too. He could hear his heart beat, for instance, and he could hear himself breathe. When he scratched his nose, he could hear the scratching sound. Still, more and more, he had the idea that he was somehow floating, like someone in a very deep pool of jet-black ink.

Then he heard more things, or thought he did. Very, very distant groaning? Errant, unintelligible words? He tried shouting; nothing seemed to issue from his throat but a frail raspy sound. He could hear air going rapidly in and out of his lungs, so that was something, at least.

He extended his arms as much as possible, hoping to feel something that made sense, like a wall or a door or some kind of support structure, but his efforts were not rewarded. He seemed to be immersed in nothing more than dead black space, and though he could hear evidence of other people distantly around him, no explanation occurred to him as to where he might actually be, nor what the circumstances were.

He was simply *existing* there.

Simply taking up space in some indefinable netherland of sheer blackness.

Time, though impossible to calculate, seemed to drag on, to the point that he, Sharsted, felt that he might very well have been here for weeks or months, with nothing—absolutely *nothing*—happening.

Those sounds he seemed to hear remained distant and vague, but then his brain started to work more subjectively, as the human brain was wont to do on certain occasions. Sharsted thought: *This is fucked up, but wouldn't it be even MORE fucked up if, all of a sudden, rotten hands reached out and started poking my face, and then lips went right against my ear and screamed?*

That's pretty much what happened exactly after the thought popped into his mind.

Hands shot out of the inestimable blackness and began to paw at his face, feeling, poking around, much as a blind person might feel someone else's face in order to "see" it. But these hands weren't rotten; they were only cool and very dry, and there seemed to be desperation in their movements, as if their owner were frantic to verify that Sharsted was genuinely present.

They went on feeling, poking, and pinching, and they did not limit their sightless investigation to Sharsted's face. They moved down the front of his neck, down his chest, and even pawed around between his legs. Worse than that came next: an unseen mouth opened near his face, licking his eyes, nose, cheeks, then sucked over his lips. Eventually, the tongue burrowed into Sharsted's mouth, roving around his oral cavity as if it needed reassurance that there was something alive inside.

And next?

Another set of lips pressed against his ear and shrieked as high and as loud as a train whistle, and—

—and Sharsted awoke, close to screaming, in the more familiar and less terrifying darkness of his own bedroom. Sharp, knife-tip-like pains flared around his heart.

Fuck! Am I dying? and he fell out of bed— *THUNK!*—over-reaching for his cellphone. When he finally found the phone, the chest pains subsided. He'd meant to dial 911.

Fuck...FUCK! he thought when his heart stopped thumping hard. *What an awful nightmare! Fuck this shit!*

Sharsted was old, or if not old, no longer young. He'd long adapted to living by himself because he knew he was too selfish for any woman to bother with, and that was fine. But he felt ancient when he dragged himself off the floor and hobbled over to get some water.

What now? he wondered, because he knew that after a nightmare of such intensity, he'd never get back to sleep. He gulped and glanced around the murky crypt-quiet confines of his apartment, half expecting to see ghosts. One day, perhaps, he'd even see his own.

It wasn't even midnight when the dream had kicked him out of sleep. He dressed and left; though not a sentiment he often felt, he thought it best to be around some other people, and fortunately his favorite Chinese restaurant, Zung Fuzhou, was open till three a.m.

Only ten minutes' walking got him there and soon he was sitting at the front bar, a place where he always felt content. The entire establishment gave him tranquility, as he was someone pretty much sick of the present and much more comfortable recollecting the past.

Zung Fuzhou was one of those rare old-school Chinese restaurants like what he remembered from the '60s and '70s: crimson wallpaper augmented by gold trellis-work, dark red carpet boasting dragons, smiling Buddhas everywhere, and a sprawling mural in the dining room of Hong Kong before the Communists had taken it back.

Even at this hour, the dining room was half full. But only one other customer occupied the lounge area. Sharsted looked at himself, a morose stick-figure, in the bright mirror panels behind the liquor shelves, where flamboyant drinks like Zombies and Suffering Bastards were made with regularity. Sharsted ordered a bottle of Tsing Tao and a traditional little glass. Those little glasses made the beer seem to last longer.

The manager—whose name was Tony, but everyone called him Kung Fu—greeted Sharsted with his usual gushing gratitude, and then Sharsted ordered "the usual," a plate of rumaki and salt and pepper squid.

"Ah, so you've ordered the rumaki," said the bar's only other customer. He was an odd pear-shaped man of indeterminate age, wearing a white shirt and red tie, with a dark gun-brush moustache but only remnant wisps of gray hair on an otherwise bald scalp. The man was so overweight it made Sharsted think of Wimpy on Popeye.

"It's the only place I know of in the county that

still serves it," Sharsted remarked of the comment. "I guess most people don't like it—younger people, I mean. They can't get past the idea of chicken livers. But me? I'll eat it all day long."

That's when he noticed that this other man—who was, as mentioned, profoundly overweight—had ordered rumaki himself, along with a pile of pork fried rice and the Twice Cooked Pork.

Damn, Sharsted thought. *Is he gonna eat all that?*

"Same here," said the man. "I like authenticity. Rumaki, along with Dim Sum and Moo Goo Gai Pan, are about the only items you'll find in a real Chinese restaurant in China. Everything else is American bastardizations. For instance, in China, you'll find no Sweet and Sour Pork, no Shrimp and Lobster Sauce, no General Tso Chicken."

Sharsted raised a brow. "Really? I didn't know that."

"Take my word for it, it's true." But then "Wimpy" cut a grin. "However, there really *was* a General Tso, in the mid-'1800s. He was among China's most skilled field commanders, and there's an interesting story that goes along with him, but you might not want to hear it while you're eating."

Sharsted shrugged. "I'm not squeamish, if that's what you mean. What's the story?"

"Okay, you asked for it. Around 1850, the

Russians—the historical enemies of China—had a habit of sending troops across the border and raiding Chinese villages. I mean, they would kill men, women and children without compunction. Well, whenever these incursions happened, the emperor would send the lauded General Tso to take care of business, as I believe the right saying goes. He'd take 20,000 or so men, outflank the Russians, and slaughter them in place. Then they'd build great fires and—can you guess? They'd *roast* the Russian soldiers and have a veritable feast."

Sharsted's face seemed to lengthen. "You mean... they *ate*—"

"Yes, indeed. They *ate* the Russian soldiers, and they ate heartily. Sometimes for days. Then, when they were finished, all those Chinese soldiers would go over the border into Russia, and... can you guess what they did?"

Sharsted drew a blank. "Uh, why, no."

"They'd stand side by side, 20,000 of them, and then they'd squat and, well, make bowel movements. It was like a calling card. Next day, the Russian reinforcements would discover 20,000 piles of excrement fringing their border. It was as if the Chinese were saying, 'If you come into our country, we will not only slaughter you, but we will *eat* you. We will *feast* on your brave soldiers. We will *nourish ourselves* on their flesh, and then we will *push* your once gallant troops out of our assholes.' After a few of these demonstrations, you can bet that the Russians, *never again* crossed that border. A fairly effective tactic—ah, but I can see you don't believe me. No matter; it's true nonetheless. And, though there never really was a dish called General Tso Chicken, there very well may have been a dish called General Tso *Human*."

Sharsted chuckled, and made a "cheers" gesture with his glass. "A captivating story to say the least."

"Despite its morbidity, cannibalism has gone on since the beginning of humankind. And it was considered a legitimate mode of revenge. When your enemy offends you, *eat* your enemy, and then enjoy the satisfaction of pushing him out your ass the next day. The *perfect* terror tactic, the *perfect* act of vengeance, the *perfect* middle finger. Don't you think?"

Sharsted, though he supposed he had to agree, was flabbergasted by the unlikelihood of this wee-hour conversation. Of course, he'd read of historical cannibalism more than once, and even cases of American troops eating Japanese troops upon hearing that the Japanese had field orders to cook and consume the flesh of American prisoners in work camps.

"It's the oldest law in history, an eye for an

eye," cited Wimpy. "Fuck with me, and I'll fuck with you worse, and then maybe you'll learn your lesson. And if you don't heed this warning, *you'll be the next pile of feces on the ground...*"

"Yes, uh, that's some lesson," Sharsted remarked, unable to think of anything else. *Wow, this guy's a unique conversationalist...*

Next, Wimpy said, quite out of the blue. "That nightmare was a bummer, huh?"

Sharsted's gaze locked on him. "What do you—?"

His train of thought was interrupted Tony came in to inquire as to their satisfaction. Sharsted was prepared to lavish his standard compliments, but suddenly Tony looked past him, his perennial smile collapsing into a blank expression of fear.

"Any of you assholes move," came a voice from behind, "I'll blow your brains *and* your chicken chow mein all over this fuckin' ceiling."

click

Armed robbery, Sharsted realized. Something he'd never experienced before.

He glanced into the mirror behind the bar again. The robber looked kind of like Frank Zappa in a Misfits hoodie. But he held a large silver revolver, moving back and forth between Sharsted, Tony, and Wimpy. A huge pistol, with a bore diameter probably large enough to admit an adult human thumb.

Fuck, Sharsted thought baldly.

The tip of the revolver nudged him; a plastic bag was handed over. "Wallet and cellphone. In the bag."

Sharsted was short of breath from the unexpected terror. "Yes, of course," he said, putting his wallet and phone in the bag. The bag said WE APPRECIATE YOUR BUSINESS! HAVE A NICE DAY, and there was a smiley face on it.

"You're smart for a useless old fuck." The robber next thrust the bag at Tony, who stood behind the bar with his hands up. "You. Charlie Chan. Unless you're sick of serving egg rolls and Poo-Poo platters, put your phone and wallet in the bag."

This Tony did with a paling face.

"Now pass it down to Mr. Potato Head over there."

He was referring to Wimpy. But, as Tony commenced to taking the bag over, there resounded a great SLAP!

Sharsted didn't know what happened; he was too busy being shit-scared, but from the corner of his eye, he saw the robber fly off his feet and slam back-first against the red and gold wall. A plume of blood seemed to eject from his lips, and teeth launched out of his mouth. The pistol clattered to the floor and landed in front of the carry-out station.

What the fuck was THAT?

Now the perpetrator lay crumpled and unconscious on the floor.

"What the fruck?" Tony exclaimed.

Wimpy stood up and pointed right at Sharsted. "Wow! Did you see that?! That brave man right there just knocked the robber out cold!"

Did I? Sharsted thought in a jumble of confusion. *Wait, no. No I didn't...*

Tony giggled. "You hero! You save us from this preece of shit!"

"No, really, I di–" Sharsted began, but at the same moment Wimpy looked him right in the eye, shook his head no, and held up an index finger as if to denote something like *Keep quiet. I'll explain later.*

Tony was nearly apoplectic with excitement. He grinned hugely at Sharsted and celebrated, "You maybe srave my life! And that guy too, and maybe even whole dining room! From now on, you eat here for free!"

Oh, man. "Thanks, Tony, but that's not nec–"

Tony would hear none of it. As he called the police, then gallantly picked up the gun and held it on the collapsed and unconscious robber, Sharsted crunched down the rest of his rumaki with slumped shoulders.

"Some night, huh?" said Wimpy, and winked.

The police came, took statements, and dragged the perpetrator off in handcuffs. An attractive blonde from the newspaper snapped a photo of Sharsted.

"That him right there!" Tony said, pointing. "He a *hero!*"

When Sharsted dejectedly opened his fortune cookie, it read TODAY YOU WILL MEET SOMEONE WHO WILL CHANGE YOUR LIFE.

But when he looked to the other end of the bar, "Wimpy" was no longer to be seen.

Next day, Sharsted awoke immersed in as much, if not more, confusion than he'd experienced the previous night.

He hoped perhaps it had all been a dream, until he turned on his computer and saw the local news headlines on the AOL page. HEROIC LOCAL MAN THWARTS ARMED ROBBER AT CHINESE RESTAURANT.

You gotta be shitting me, he thought, rubbing his eyes.

There was a bright digital pic of Sharsted

smiling ineptly from his barstool, right in front of his rumaki and salt-and-pepper squid. Tony grinned behind him, hamming it up for the camera. Another pic showed the police stuffing a very groggy Frank Zappa into the back of a cruiser.

Oh, well...

Sharsted, retired now, tended to sit around most of the time, watching Tubi because it was free. He settled in to watch *Amityville Karen, Amityville Emmanuel,* and *Amityville Wet T-Shirt Contest.* Even solitary men of Sharsted's age felt the urge to masturbate on occasion but Sharsted resisted the impulse... until the last girl in *Amityville Wet T-Shirt Contest* took off her top...

Ridiculous, he thought, throwing out the kleenex. Could hackers infiltrate his cable line and somehow watch him through the TV screen? The prospect sounded impossible but he'd read of such things many times. *Fuck it. Who cares?*

At about 7 p.m., there was a knock at the door.

Can't they see the No Soliciting sign? He HATED IT when people knocked on his door. *There's NO REASON for ANYONE to be KNOCKING ON MY DOOR!*

He grumbled going to the door, then looked in the peephole.

What the FUCK?

It was the overweight guy from the bar last night. It was "Wimpy."

Sharsted opened the door, his mouth agape.

"We meet again!' Wimpy said. "How's everything going, Mr. Sharsted?"

Sharsted never told the guy his name; no doubt he read it in the news article. But—

"How do you know where I live?" he asked suspiciously.

"Oh, I, uh, got your address out of the book."

Do phone books even still exist? "Yeah?"

"Great picture of you in the paper, by the way." Wimpy winked. "I suppose you can thank me for that."

Sharsted could only remain standing there, his mouth open, his hand on the knob.

"Aren't you gonna invite me in?" Another wink. "I'm not a vampire."

Sharsted stalled, then stepped back and let the man enter.

"Wimpy" waltzed right in, looking around the drab apartment. "Maid's day off, right—no. I'm just kidding." He looked out the patio window. "So I'm sure you're aware that something was seriously messed up last night."

Sharsted managed, "You might say that…"

"*I'm* the one who knocked the robber out, but you must know that already."

"That's impossible. I was there, remember? You were at least fifteen feet away when that asshole hit the floor. Now, I know *I* didn't do it, but there was no way *you* could have… unless you have— what's the word?—telekinetic powers."

"I have telekinetic powers," said Wimpy, nonchalantly.

"Is that a fact?"

"But it's no big deal." Now the weird man was browsing around the kitchen. "And my name's not Wimpy, by the way. I mean, I know I'm fat but—wow. What an insult."

The scenario was jumbling the threads of Sharsted's thought processes. *Okay, okay, wait a minute… What's going on here?* "The only way you could know I thought of you as Wimpy is if you're psychic."

"I'm psychic as well as telekinetic. Among other things." He opened some cabinets. "Do you have any peanut butter?"

"No. What's going on? This is fucked up," Sharsted said, straining his patience.

"That's what I'm here to tell you. And, in case you want to know, my name's Raguel." The man's eyes lit up at a cupboard. "Can I have some of this Fiddle Faddle?"

"Sure," Sharsted muttered. "So, Raguel? A foreign name, I take it? Where are you from?"

The man, Raguel, winced when he ate a handful of Fiddle Faddle. "This stuff's stale! Close the bag up each time. Get some of those clamp things."

"Where are you from?" Sharsted asked again.

"You might say I'm from the fields of the nephilim." Raguel chuckled. "I'm kidding. But you're not quite ready to believe where I'm really from, not yet. By morning, you probably will be. Come on, let's get out of here. This place is a dump."

"Thanks very much…"

The entrance to Sharsted's apartment complex was on a street called Seminole Boulevard; a major road north, it passed many restaurants, bars, and strip malls.

Raguel had assumed the navigational duties. Before them, the straight, dark thoroughfare extended in a vanishing point into a stop-light-flecked infinity. Raguel turned at the next corner. But just as Sharsted would ask where they were going, they stopped short at the sight of multiple police cars clogging the road. Sharsted took one close look and uttered, "Holy shit…"

It was a traffic accident—not uncommon in this area at night. A wheelchair sat toppled over and crushed. Just as crushed, some twenty feet away, lay the wheelchair's owner: askew in the road with knees and elbows bent at unnatural angles and his neck distorted. The man's head could've been a smashed cantaloupe centered over a great shining halo of black blood.

"Hit and run," Raguel said under his breath.

"That's fuckin' awful. If the driver gets away, that's proof to me that there's no God." It was an uncharacteristic comment from Sharsted—he almost never spoke of such opinions in front of others, but this time the words exited his mouth without forethought.

Raguel's smirk warped to a tight, half-smile. "Everything evens out in the end," he said, slipping something out of his pocket.

Sirens could be heard in the distance; an ambulance, no doubt. Sharsted was not into rubber-necking but something insisted that he look as the crushed victim: a rag-tag white guy perhaps in his '30s. The size of the pool of blood shouted at Sharsted; he couldn't imagine a single person contained so much blood. But outrage seized him when he glanced back at Raguel.

"You're shitting me! You're taking pictures of a dead guy?"

At first, it appeared so. Raguel had produced something that looked like a brass cigarette case, but, when opened, the device purveyed small round lenses on one side and two tiny eyeholes on the other.

"It's not a camera," Raguel muttered aside, looking through the eyeholes.

Sharsted recalled seeing similar things, like opera glasses or mini binoculars, often for sale at yard sales or junk shops. Still…

"So what the fuck are you looking at? The guy's dead. Don't tell me you're one of those ghouls who gets off eyeballing corpses."

"This is called a Lente Blasphemia, Model 7-A7," Raguel said, and handed it to Sharsted. "Look at the dead guy."

Sharsted hesitantly took the cigarette-case-looking device and brought it to his eyes. Then…

What the fuck is THIS shit?

At first he thought it must really be one of those VR viewer things that you wore like glasses to watch movies and play games. But what he saw was no movie or game. He saw no crushed wheelchair, no dead person with a crushed head in the road—in fact, he saw no road at all. What he saw instead was something akin to a movie scene, and…

It was just… *abominable.*

A scrawny young man knelt in the woods. His pants were down. Along with other junk such as wheel-less bicycles, some deflated tires on bent rims, and some rotten suitcases lying opened and empty, there was a rusted bathtub-lining full of a goulash of black water and dead leaves.

The young man was on his knees before the tub, sporting a throbbing erection. With him was a naked adolescent girl, and he was holding her head under the bathtub water. He let her up a few times just as she was about to drown, then pushed her head right back in. After several cycles of this, his victim went limp. The scrawny man wasted no time in raping the girl from behind with her head still submerged in the water.

Sharsted tingled in morbid shock, on the verge of vomiting. He handed the device back to Raguel. "What the FUCK was that?"

"Past deeds." Raguel pointed to the corpse in the street. "Just the tip of the iceberg for that gentleman, believe me. He'd raped and/or murdered at least a dozen little girls, until he got shot in a drug deal that went bad. Paralyzed from the waist down. Poor guy, huh? Boo-hoo. I only wish we could've gotten to him a lot sooner."

Sharsted's ire was *brimming* in him. "What the fuck are you talking about, man? Are you telling me that those opera glasses show a person's past?"

"Yeah." Raguel recommenced walking. "Past or future. It's selectable."

"Sorry, but I have to call bullshit on that. How did you rig it?"

Raguel shrugged. "The Lente Blasphemia, Model 7-A7, can show a person's past or future— his sins, I mean. His worst crimes." He stalled. "Sorry, I'm being politically incorrect. I should say *his or her* past. Or… *their* past. I'm not all that hip to the pronoun stuff. I'm old school."

Sharsted followed the corpulent man's giant-avocado-shaped shadow. "This is fuckin' crazy!" He couldn't maintain a coherent line of thought. And there was something else, wasn't there? "And what was that you said last night? Something about my nightmare? I don't believe that you knew about my nightmare."

"Why not? When you asked me if I was psychic, I told you the truth. I said yes."

Sharsted stomped on after him. "Okay, then what was my nightmare?"

"You seemed to be floating in a completely lightless place. You could see *nothing* in any direction, yes? And you thought you could hear people talking or even screaming from far off. Am I close?"

Fuck, Sharsted thought. *Am I going nuts? Is this what insanity is like? Is this guy a hallucination?*

"Let's go in here!" Raguel said, beaming. It was a bar/restaurant with a sign that read CAPT. SALTY'S. AUCE SHRIMP—15 DOLLARS. 2-POUND LOBSTER RAFFLE TONIGHT!

"Shit, man. This place is a redneck dive."

"Come on, maybe we'll win a lobster!"

Sharsted followed him in to the dark catacomb-like establishment. Loud, shitty music; drunk rednecks in ball caps eating fries and fried shrimp, guys playing pool, tramps smoking cigarettes under the NO SMOKING signs, baseball on the TV's.

"Let's sit at the bar!" Raguel's big face grinned. "It's more slice-of-life, isn't it?"

"I guess…" They both pulled up seats at the bar.

A dilapidated blond barmaid with dark circles under her eyes walked right up. She had *magnificent* breasts but that was about it. "My name's Marcie. What'll it be?"

"Two drafts, plus whatever you want on me," Raguel said.

"Why, how sweet!"

"You better hope they don't have Louis XIII here. That stuff's a hundred bucks a shot," Sharsted pointed out.

"If they do, I can afford it. But she'll probably get herself a Fireball. I much prefer beer—it's the oldest alcoholic beverage on Earth. There's history in every sip."

"Whatever. So, tell me—"

"Be patient. Strive for the patience of Job, it's a very positive character trait," said Raguel. "I'll begin with a quote. 'Remember this night, for it is the beginning of forever.' It's Dante." He looked right at Sharsted.

"Okay. Big deal."

"You're so naive, oblivious, and linear-thinking that you won't believe anything I say at first."

Am I? Sharsted wondered. *I'm naive, oblivious and linear-thinking?* He thought this was too severe an assessment.

"The nightmare you had wasn't really a nightmare. It was a vision of the future. You were in Purgatory—that's what the place is like. You're not a *bad* person, but you're not exactly the greatest person, either. You're not bad enough to go to Hell when you die, but not good enough to go to Heaven. Here's your chance to change that. Very, very few people get a chance like this."

The beers were set down: Busch Light in plastic cups. Sharsted was so mentally disarrayed right now that he didn't even shoot a glance at the barmaid's spectacular cleavage, but *not* so mentally disarrayed that he forgot to frown when he took his first sip of the tepid beer.

"Care to buy into the lobster raffle, sweetie?"

Marcie asked. "It's only five bucks."

"Certainly, my dear." Like magic, Raguel produced a five-dollar bill and handed it to her. In return, she gave him a ticket. "I'm feeling very lucky tonight, Marcie. I'll bet I win."

"Maybe but probably not," she informed him. "Over a dozen people have already entered."

"Ah, then we shall see, won't we?"

What the hell is going on here? Sharsted thought. *And what am I doing sitting here with this fruitloop?* "You were saying? Very few people get a chance like this? A chance like what?"

Raguel drained half his beer in one swig. "A chance to assure yourself a place in Heaven when you die."

"But how could you possibly know that? You know when I'm going to die?"

"I do."

"When?"

"I'm not obliged to say." Raguel returned his gaze to Sharsted. "You *do* believe in God, right?"

Sharsted's nose crinkled up. "I don't know. Yeah. Probably not. Maybe. Uh. Probably."

"That's a start, I suppose."

"What? You can tell by looking in the binocular thing when someone's going to die?"

"No, no, no. The Lente Blasphemia is just an identification tool. It shows us the transgressions of a person's past and future, as well as their inherent mature. We use it to make *determinations*."

"Determinations, huh?" Sharsted was now sitting with his elbow on the bar and his chin in his palm.

"I'm a Caliginaut, Mr. Sharsted," came Raguel's next abstruse statement. "You don't know what that is, so I'll tell you. A Caliginaut is a particular kind of angel—"

"Oh, so you're an *angel*. Now I get it."

"Like any *system*, there's a system in Heaven. It's a bit like a lot of governments today but we call it The Triquetra."

"Triquetra," Sharsted murmured. "Oh, yeah, I've heard of it."

"The executive branch, representative branch, and judicial branch. That's how you can think of it. First, of course, there's the executive arm. There's—you know. The Guy, the Dude, the One Up Top, running the show. God, if you will. And there's no voting Him in or out. He's in for good."

"Some democracy—"

"I never said it was a democracy!" Raguel snapped. "We've merely adopted some of the armature of that system of rule. But of course, God can't be subject to re-election. That would be absurd and an affront to logic. After all, God is the only perfect entity. He created everything."

Sharsted flapped a hand. "Okay, fine."

"Good. You were beginning to annoy me." Raguel glared a bit. "But, like I was saying, there's three parts. The second is something like a representative branch—Congress, Parliament, that sort of thing. And the third, the judiciary—the Caliginauts are part of *that*."

"Judges," Sharsted supposed, going along with the inane conversation.

"In a sense, yes. We do God's dirty work. We're his ministers of righteousness and the transitive enemies of the Adversary."

Sharsted finished his first beer—it was terrible, skunky—and ordered another. *I've got nothing better to do, so why not listen?*

Raguel continued. "It goes in cycles. Here, congressmen are elected every two years, senators every six. The old are often voted out and replaced by the new."

"I know. I did go to school a long time ago—"

"Well, in Heaven there are voting cycles too," Raguel said, but was looking around at all the dull patrons. "Ever noticed how the first fifty years of the 20th century were exponentially worse than the second fifty years? In the first fifty you had the two worst and most deadly wars in history. Multiple economic collapses, the dust bowl, the locust plague, and the Spanish Influenza pandemic that killed more people than the Black Death. Stuff like that. But in the second fifty, sure, there were wars, outbreaks of disease, rising dictators and all. But it was a drop in the bucket compared to those first fifty or so years, right?"

Sharsted sipped more beer, thought about it, sipped more beer, then said, "Yeah, I guess."

"Well, see, our cycles periodically change. A new Celestial Parliament was voted in in about 1950."

"What you're saying is the dumbest thing I've ever heard," Sharsted muttered.

"To you, yes. You're finite-minded. You're *human.*"

"And you're not?"

"No, I told you, I'm—"

"You're an *angel.*"

"A Caliginaut–"

Marcie the bar maid stepped up to announce, "We'll be drawing the raffle winner in a few minutes! Keep your fingers crossed."

"We will, indeed," Raguel told her with enthusiasm.

But Sharsted had barely heard her. This time he *was* staring at her seductive cleavage and big braless breasts with conical nipples poking against the fabric of her tight ZZ Top t-shirt.

Damn, he thought.

Raguel frowned at him. "Really, Mr. Sharsted. At least *try* to resist such impulses. Lust is a sin."

Sharsted darted a brief glance at Raguel's enormous stomach, thighs, and love-handles. "So is gluttony, right?"

Raguel's affable expression crumbled. "That's very offensive, Mr. Sharsted. I'm doing you a favor, remember? It's uncalled for to insult me."

"Sorry. I was just countering your statement by pointing out a glaring contradiction."

Raguel shook his head rather ruefully. "A thousand years ago, I would've sent you packing for that comment. And some of my cohorts would've done far worse."

This was getting amusing. "Like how?"

"Like letting you be captured by Tatars in Crimea. Do you have any idea what they did to the penises of captured invaders?"

Penises, thought Sharsted in a nebulous fog.

"Okay, I apologize for implying that you're guilty of the sin of gluttony—" He shot another quick glance at his escort's belly anyway."So, you can continue with this impossible monologue."

"Very well. As I was saying, there are voting cycles in Heaven just as there are here. The Celestial Parliamentary elections are one such example. But we Caliginauts exist in the Empyrean Court. The Parliament changes the laws in various

Resolutions. This happened very recently. And now we, the members of the Empyrean Court, have had our duty assignments changed. We're now allowed to alter the future for the benefit of the treatise of Good Will. Follow me so far?"

"Sure," Sharsted said and ordered his third beer. "Alter the future."

"Over the millennia, it's switched back and forth several times. For the time being, at least, we're allowed to, well, balance things out, monkey with the scales, so to speak. We're allowed to nip things in the bud. You'll understand more as we go along."

What am I DOING with this guy? Sharsted asked himself. *I should be sitting on my ass at home watching Julie Anne Prescott movies on Tubi, but instead--*

"We've been given permission to nip them in the bud now, Mr. Sharsted," Raguel continued with his little disquisition. "Sure, the sociological conclusions of the day tell you that, for lack of a better term, bad people aren't *born,* they're *made.* Is that your understanding?"

Sharsted's chin was back in his palm. "Of course. Serial-killers, rapists, etc., become criminals because of their upbringing or because of aspects of their life experience. They can't help the way they are because they're actually victims of negative environments, mostly during their childhoods. If a little kid is raped by his stepfather, uncle, teacher, whatever, then that's the reason that he becomes a rapist in adulthood. If a little girl is tricked out by her drug-addict, prostitute mother, then the little girl becomes a drug-addict and prostitute herself later in life. And on and on. Kids grow up to sell drugs in the ghetto because that's what their mothers and father did. The indoctrination of learned behavior. You grow up in a criminal environment, you become a criminal yourself. It's a simple logic and it makes sense."

"So monsters are made, not born?"

"Yes."

Raguel raised a finger. "And *that* is where you're wrong, Mr. Sharsted. Believe me, some people are simply born evil. It's one of the Devil's most effective machinations, along with the proliferation of pop psychology and sociology. Satan goes to great efforts to see to it that some children are *born* evil. They are *born* to become acolytes of Lucifer and to do his diabolical bidding. You might not *want* to believe that, but you can trust me. It's quite true and it's a harrowing circumstance, particularly for the voting members of the Celestial Parliament. For the longest time, it was the biggest question on the floor: why not stop it in advance? And it always got voted down. But times change, Mr. Sharsted, there just like here. Now we're allowed to stop it before the damage is done." Raguel grinned, repeating, "We're allowed to nip them in the bud."

Sharsted shook his head rapidly, like a cartoon character. "You mean… you're allowed to kill *kids* before they grow up to be rapists and murderers?"

"Well, yes, but not just kids. Anyone. Anyone who was born evil. It's one thing to be born ignorant of the Gospels. But it's quite another to *know* the Gospels and then to reject them with a vengeance; it's just more of Satan's tactics. But now we can fight back. And if it doesn't work?" Raguel shrugged. "It'll get voted out and they'll think of something else."

Sharsted noticed a pregnant woman yapping by one of the pool tables; she wore a t-shirt that read LEGGO MY PREGGO!

"Ah, I see you're lusting after that pregnant woman," Raguel said.

"I'm not *lusting!*"

"Well, let's see…" Careful to keep his hands wrapped around the cigarette-case looking thing, he raised it to his eyes and took a quick peek, then put it away. "Ah, I'm happy to say your pregnant friend was *not* born evil, but—"

"You've gotta be shitting me!" Sharsted objected. "You're telling me that you work for *God*, and *God* says it's okay to kill people before they commit horrific acts?"

"No, no, I said the *Celestial Parliament* did. God does give His subjects some leeway in the department of home rule. We're not puppets, you know—"

Sharsted ground his teeth. "That *ridiculous!*"

Raguel had no time to counter the statement when Marcie rang the tip bell and loudly informed, "Listen up, folks, and get your tickets out. It's time to pick the raffle winner!"

Excited murmurs rose as all eyes looked anxiously toward the barmaid.

"And the winner is..." Marcie began, "Seven seven, seven seven seven, seven seven."

The excited murmurs collapsed to groans of disappointment and then the losing tickets were dropped on the floor.

"I won!" Raguel exclaimed, holding up his ticket.

Sharsted looked cock-eyed at him.

Marcie, grinning, took the ticket. "So you did, sir. Do you want your lobster stuffed and baked or steamed?"

"Hmm, let me see... I'll take it stuffed and baked, please. And make it to go if you don't mind."

"Yes, sir. Congratulations!"

Sharsted was still looking cockeyed at the obese man. "Did you... *rig* that?"

"I wouldn't go so far as to say that."

"You did, didn't you?" Sharsted glared in amazement. "You used some kind of angel voodoo to make yourself win."

Raguel smirked. "Mr. Sharsted, please don't change the subject. We're not talking about lobsters, we're talking about your destiny."

"My *destiny?*"

"Don't you want to go to Heaven when you die?"

The question struck Sharsted as just more bombast. "This is *bullshit—*"

"No, this is a *gift.* As it stands now, it you died this moment, you would go to Purgatory. Now, how long you remain in Purgatory depends on you." Raguel leveled his eyes on Sharsted. "You'll be there until you sufficiently reconcile yourself with God, and accept the holy sacrifice of His Son. Could be a week, could be a thousand years. I don't know."

Sharsted simply sat there with his jaw hanging.

"Or," Raguel continued, "you can accept this gift with your whole heart and bypass Purgatory and, in the long run, save quite a few innocent people from horrific torment, death, and torture. Now, you've seen Purgatory. Your dream the other night?"

Sharsted stared further at the preposterous overweight man. Indeed, he remembered the dream, the nightmare, all-too-well, and the recollection seemed to slam-dunk his sentience into a morose lugubrious chasm. He didn't want to ever see that place again, and since Raguel seemed to know about the dream via some psychic kinship, maybe…

Maybe this ISN'T bullshit. Maybe this is real, and maybe he really IS what he says he is…

"Yes," Sharsted said in a grave voice. "I remember Purgatory and I don't want to go there."

"Excellent! Now you're starting to see the light." Raguel smiled in some self-satisfaction. "So you agree to the terms?"

Sharsted winced. "What terms?"

Raguel's eyes twinkled. "I give you assignments. You carry those assignments out. And when you die, you go to Heaven. It's pretty cut and dry."

Sharsted, by now, was finding it easier and easier to put two and two together. *Nipping them in the bud…* "So I go to Heaven when I die, but for that I gotta *murder* bad people?"

"That's correct. There's a lot of gray area relative to your use of the word *murder* but, yes. You kill who I tell you to kill, the way I tell you to kill them, and you're… in like Flynn, as I believe the right saying goes." Then he finished his next beer.

Think, think! Sharsted pleaded with himself. *Do I really believe this? This is impossible, right?* But he *had* seen a younger version of the Wheelchair Guy drowning and raping a little girl when he'd looked into the binocular things. How could that be possible without supernatural facilitation? And Raguel had described his nightmare in crystal clarity. *Coincidence?*

"I see," Raguel remarked. "You need more convincing–"

"Yeah."

"When you were seven years old, two bullies named Dicky McAvoy and Jim Meyers tied you to a tree with a dog chain, pulled your pants down, peed on you, and then threw dirt clods at you. Did you ever tell anyone that?"

Sharsted felt instantly dizzy. "N-no."

"You never told your parents?"

"No, because they said if I did they'd—"

"They'd kill your parents and your dog." Raguel's expression compressed in some obscure frustration. "But I can't for the life of me remember the dog's name."

Sharsted felt like he was sinking. "It was King," he croaked.

"Yes, the collie! And when you were in eighth grade, in Mrs. Christianson's science class, you—"

"No!"

"—you masturbated *in class,* under your desk at the back of the room."

"You can't possible know that!" Sharsted snapped, loudly enough to turn a few heads.

"Take it easy, Mr. Sharsted," Raguel whispered. "Don't cause a scene."

Sharsted whispered fiercely, "You'd have jerked off in class too if you had to look at *her* brick shithouse tits and body every day!"

"No, Mr. Sharsted, I assure you I wouldn't have. Why? Because I'm an angel who has committed himself to an eternity of serving God. I've willed myself to be incognizant of lust." The rotund man tapped a finger on the bar. "When you were twelve years old, you stole model paints from the People's Drug Store on Route 197 and—" Raguel chuckled. "– you got caught."

"Okay!" Sharsted rushed the word. "I believe you!"

"Superb. Now, I'll ask you again. Do you agree to the terms?"

Even though he knew it was impossible, Sharsted also knew that Raguel was for real. *My destiny. To go to Heaven...* "I gotta tell ya, this sounds more and more like a trick. Like it's a deal with the Devil, and when I agree, you'll sprout horns and a tail."

"I give you my word as a deacon of the Lord Almighty, Mr. Sharsted, that no such thing is the case. I'm *incapable* of deceit, I *cannot* lie. So… time's a-wastin', as I believe the right saying goes. Are you in or out?"

Sharsted felt numb from head to toe when he said, "I'm in."

Raguel's bulbous face beamed. "Then let's be on our merry way." He put a $100 bill on the bar and squeezed off his stool.

"What about your lobster?" Sharsted pointed out.

Raguel shrugged. "No time, I'm afraid. Our enchanting barmaid can have it. I'm sure she works hard."

Sharsted shook his head with a frown and followed the man out.

He hadn't previously taken note that the pregnant woman had left before them, but there she was now, at the corner of the building, smoking a cigarette.

"She shouldn't be smoking while she's pregnant," Sharsted couldn't help but object.

"No, she shouldn't. Satan has blighted God's Green Earth with untold admixtures of evil. People are people, I'm afraid, and often they're victimized by such blights. Just the way Lucifer wants it." Then Raguel remained where he stood.

Sharsted's brain began to tick with a grim consideration. "Wait, wait, don't tell me I have to *kill* a pregnant woman…"

"No, Mr. Sharsted. But, since you've agreed to the terms, you'll be expected to terminate the wicked progeny that now abodes in her belly."

Sharsted nearly fell over. "I'm *not* gonna kill a fuckin' baby, you asshole!"

"You'd be far better off to refrain from insults, Mr. Sharsted." Scowling, Raguel handed over the Lente Blasphemia. "Take a gander—as I believe the right saying goes—at the young lady's stomach."

Sharsted took the device, brought the eyeholes to his eyes, and took a "gander."

One half-second glimpse was enough to propel him backward, aghast.

What he saw was this: a room—a *classroom,* it would appear—engulfed in roaring, cracking flames. Screams wheeled about in an insane cacophony while *figures* in the flame—*small* figures in most cases—convulsed and collapsed, many in wheelchairs.

"My God…"

"Indeed," said his cohort. "When the baby in that woman's belly reaches his twenty-seventh year, he will chain all the exit doors of a school for handicapped children and then firebomb it. Do you want to prevent that event from occurring? Go ahead and take another look through the Lente Blasphemia if you feel the impetus is insufficient."

Sharsted stood all but paralyzed. He couldn't get the monstrous images out of his head.

"I didn't think so." Seemingly from out of nowhere, Raguel produced something like a carry-case, the size of a lunch box.

Sharsted snapped out of his horrified muse. "What's that?"

"You can think of it as a subcontractor's tool box. It contains all the implements you'll need to carry out the assignments you've agreed to discharge." From the box he withdrew a large hypodermic needle, which he passed to Sharsted.

"No, you don't mean I have to—"

"You will push this needle into the pregnant woman's belly and depress the plunger."

"No," Sharsted whispered with a chill.

"If you don't, all those handicapped children will be burned alive. Do the job, Mr. Sharsted. Save all those children…"

Sharsted's hand shook when he took the hypo. "She's not just gonna stand there while I stick in a needle in her fuckin' stomach! She'll scream, she'll run away. She'll call the cops and I'll get thrown in prison!"

"None of those things will happen." Raguel's patience seemed to be wavering again. "While you're such engaged, the subject of your assignment will immediately fall under a Paresis

Spell—she won't be able to move. And you'll be invisible, so she won't be able to see you and therefore she won't be able to report you to the police. In fact, she won't be able to remember any of it. You've nothing to fear. I should think that, by now, there's an unimpeachable credibility in everything I tell you."

Sharsted wasn't sure what he intended to say next because, with no volition of his own, his brain relit with the pandemonic images of all those children screaming, writhing, burning alive...

Sharsted turned like an automaton, brandishing the hypodermic. And walked right up to the pregnant woman.

She didn't see him; in fact she didn't move a muscle when Sharsted pulled her t-shirt up to expose her distended belly. The needle-tip hovered.

"Insert the needle into the baby's skull," Raguel ordered.

"I don't know when the kid's *skull* is!"

"Have faith. Just do it. Your newfound instincts as a subcontractor will guide your hand without any conscious effort on your part."

Sharsted's eyes were peeled. He bent over and leaned in. *Am I... Am I really doing this?* Then he pushed the needle into the lower half of her tight distended belly. So tight, in fact, was the shiny skin over the belly that Sharsted could see the vaguest reflection of his own face.

He pushed the needle in farther. It was a long needle and it penetrated several inches, but then stopped momentarily as if it had encountered an obstruction, then—

Sharsted almost threw up when he felt more than heard a tiny *crunch,* after which the needle went in to the hilt.

Then he emptied the hypodermic's contents, as per instructions.

Blurred vision overwhelmed him. He staggered backward as good as blind. He began to turn and retreat back to where Raguel turned but—

"You have to pull her shorts off!" Raguel barked.

"Huh?"

"Her shorts. Pull them off; otherwise the baby won't be able to come out! Don't you have any foresight at all?"

A sound like bad machine bearings filled his head. He returned to where the motionless woman stood, urged her to sit on the ground, then removed her frayed cut-off jeans and her panties. Flowery cursive writing on the front of the panties read FILL 'ER UP!

Sharsted's awareness dripped back into his head: the woman's pubic region was stubbled by Lady's Five O'clock Shadow, and even as he stared down he could see the vulva spread as the perfect orb of the fetus's head began to extrude.

Out of here, he thought dazedly. He simply could not bring himself to watch the rest.

Some indeterminate time later, he regained full sentience and found himself walking down a dark suburban street with Raguel at his side.

"You're remarkably inattentive, Mr. Sharsted," Raguel complained. "You left the needle sticking in her stomach! I had to retrieve it myself!"

"Uh," Sharsted uttered. "Oh. Sorry."

"No matter, I got it back. But please pay attention to such things in the future."

It appeared to be a nice neighborhood they were strolling through. "What are we doing here?"

"We're journeying to your next assignment," Raguel replied.

Sharsted sighed. "And where are we?"

"I believe we're in the Vinoy district of St. Petersburg." Raguel took several approving glances at the large houses they passed, and high-priced sedans. "Pretty ritzy, I see."

Alarmed, Sharsted looked at his watch; it was just past 8 p.m. "We couldn't have walked here in the short time it's been since we left the bar! Did we take a cab and I just don't remember?"

"No cab, Mr. Sharsted." Raguel seemed to hitch up his cargo shorts with some difficulty.

"And we didn't walk. Let's just say I have a knack for traversing distances while foregoing any expenditure of time."

"More angel voodoo," Sharsted mumbled.

"If you will. We're visiting the home of a wealthy executive—"

Sharsted stopped short. "And let me guess. I have to *kill* the wealthy executive before he commits some horrible atrocity in the future."

"No, no, leave it to me. The wealthy executive isn't even home now. He's having dinner with his wife downtown right now. We're going to stop by and say hello to the wealthy executive's *babysitter.*"

Sharsted nodded at his cynical best. "'Stop by and say hello' means I have to *fuckin' kill* the babysitter. Am I reading this right?"

"You're reading it with crystal clarity, Mr. Sharsted. The babysitter's name is Linda. She's an attractive blonde and quite amiable when she needs to be. She possesses the appearance of a fine young lady you wouldn't think capable of so much as a single ungodly thought." Raguel raised a finger in an ineffective attempt at relevant emphasis. "Ah, but as I believe the right saying goes: looks can be deceiving."

Sharsted shook his head at the stupid quip. "So what did Linda do?"

"You'll see when we get there."

They got there a few minutes later, a large post-art-decco-ish home with roofs slanted at various angles. Meticulous shrubbery adorned the property. Sharsted followed Raguel between two tall spires of junipers until they were both looking into the living room window.

"There she is," Raguel remarked.

Wow, thought Sharsted. *Hubba, hubba.*

It was an unseemly sight he was looking upon, but he had to admit this babysitter, Linda, was quite the looker. At this precise moment, she was standing upright, fully naked, and bent over at the waist, while a similarly naked tattoo-besmirched young man stood behind her, copulating frenetically, his ring-pierced face twisted up in the throes of anticipatory bliss.

Damn," Sharsted said. "That's some show."

"Clearly, Linda invited her boyfriend over as soon as the parents left." Raguel was shaking his head as he continued to peer in. "Expressly *without* permission of the parents, I might add."

In no long time, the tattooed guy achieved orgasm amid a fleshy exhibition of huffing, puffing, hip-gyrations, and ludicrous facial contortions.

"Damn it, Pip!" Linda snapped over his shoulder. "Can't you last more than a minute? I wanna cum too, ya know."

"Pip" sat down bare-assed on a ten-thousand-dollar Hadley Square couch. "Sorry, babe. Have to get'cha next time."

Linda turned naked and looked toward what Sharsted had only just now noticed: a baby's crib. When Sharsted squinted, he could see the baby through the crib's bars. It was—

"This is the ugliest fuckin' baby I've ever seen," Linda commented, leaning over the crib's rail. "Little silver-spoon ugly motherfucker. I *hate* rich kids." Then she reached down into the crib.

"What are you doing?" the tattooed guy asked.

"I'm gonna pinch his little dicky! Make the fat-faced little fuck cry!"

The tattooed guy chuckled. All Sharsted could see directly was Linda reaching into the crib with an intent grin on her face, evidently pinching the baby's genitals. The baby, unsurprisingly, began to wail.

"Pip! His little balls are like olives!"

"Oh, yeah? Snap a pic, put it on your Facebook!"

Linda's face pinkened with malevolence. "I can't tell you how much I want to pop both his little balls!"

"Yeah, that would be cool, but the parents would take him to the doctor's and then they'd know you did it. You won't want to do time in the lezzy tank. Believe me, I know girls who've been there. They'll turn your face into a park bench."

"Yuck!"

"But give him one more good hard pinch just for the hell of it," said the tattooed guy.

This Linda did, and burst into hideous laughter when the volume of the baby's shrill objections doubled.

"She's fucked up, all right," Sharsted said to his escort. "But I'm supposed to *kill* her for pinching a baby's cock and balls?"

"No, no, no, Mr. Sharsted," Raguel said, rolling his eyes. "You've been assigned to kill her for murdering her *own* babies several years from now. She's pure, unadulterated *evil.*" He handed Sharsted the Lente Blasphemia again.

It was with no enthusiasm that Sharsted took the arcane device and brought it to his eyes…

There was Linda, about ten years older. She was standing in what appeared to be the kitchen of a trailer, and she wore a frayed slip whose tightness and sheer material elucidated the features of her breasts. She was standing before an oven, and when she opened the oven, Sharsted could see it was filled with bright orange light and the dial on the broiler-knob read 500.

Then Linda pushed a pair of male twin babies into the oven and closed the door. Under her breath, she whispered, "Hail Satan…"

"I've seen enough!" Sharsted shouted, but when he tried to lower the Lente Blasphemia, he found he could not, not matter how hard he tried.

"It's important for you to *see*, Mr. Sharsted," came Raguel's dark, grinding response. "Your tasks are not fleeting—you need to take this *seriously*. The lives of those twins depend on it."

Sharsted shivered in place. His hands could not lower the Lente Blasphemia. Some force—no doubt some force executed by Raguel—kept his eyes glued to the eyeholes.

The muffled sounds coming from the oven defied sane description, but then, after several minutes of standing there, smiling at the skin-crawling noise, Linda reopened the oven, to reveal two bright-orange, blistering, twitching lumps whose faces were bubbling and whose tiny mouths were jerking open and closed. Now that the infantile shrieks of horror had subsided, the only sound to be heard was something like hissing steam.

Sharsted felt unable to close his eyes when he handed the Lente Blasphemia back. "How should I do it?"

"Any way you want," Raguel said good-naturedly. He smiled. "Be resourceful."

Sharsted walked with deliberation to the front

door. He heard the door unlock before he touched the knob, and next he was walking across the cool dark foyer.

First he went to the kitchen, selected a particularly sharp knife from a drawer, then moved quietly to the living room, where Linda, still naked, was harping at her tattooed miscreant boyfriend,

"Damn it, Pip! I told you! You can't smoke pot in here! The Delanys will smell it when they get home, then I lose a perfectly good babysitting job!"

The tattooed guy shrugged and fired up his bowl anyway. Sharsted stood right before the both of them but they obviously couldn't see him. He looked down at the baby in the crib, who'd piped down now that Linda had taken her hand out of his diapers. He smiled at the baby, made a *coochie-coo* gesture with his finger, then turned, By now Linda had frozen in place, no doubt due to Raguel Paresis Spell. He walked right up to Linda and—-

"What the—?" the boyfriend said, gaping.

—-slit her throat with a single, forceful slash, from the back of her neck to her adam's apple.

The product of the act might be called spectacular, as six-foot-long lines of blood jettisoned from the wound across the room, spoiling the plush, pricey ash-gray carpet. Linda's eyes and mouth locked open in speechless shock. She slapped a hand to her throat but to no avail; the blood continued to spurt energetically between her fingers, and as she turned, the last few spurts hit the tattooed guy in the face, then in the chest, and then right in his genitals.

Linda collapsed.

That's what I'm talking about, Sharsted thought. He dropped the knife and exited the house.

"Well done, well done!" Raguel celebrated. "Not even an inkling of hesitancy!"

"Uh, yeah."

"Now those twins will never be born, never will suffer the incogitable agonies you witnessed. They will not be fodder for Satan." Raguel smiled with satisfaction. "You serve God well."

Sharsted made a face. *God,* he thought. *Really?* "So you're telling me that *God* greenlights this stuff? It's okay with him that I caused an innocent women to miscarry and then slit a teenaged girl's throat? I thought God was all loving, that God loves everyone, that all people are the children of God."

"Oh, that's quite true, but you need to read a little more of the Bible. God's not terribly patient and He's got a short temper. In the wink of an eye, God incinerated Sodom and Gomorrah. In one night, He killed all the first-born male children of Egypt. Through the mouth of His Son, He cursed

Chorazin, Bethsaida, and Capernaum, and to this day they *remain* cursed."

"God gets pissed sometimes, in other words," Sharsted said.

"Oh, yes, and who can blame Him? Humans should feel lucky that God hasn't abandoned the Earth altogether, just swipe His hand and clear the planet off. Start again. Believe me, Mr. Sharsted, several times a year the Archangels implore Him to do just that."

"Okay, then what happened back there?" He pointed his thumb behind him. "I just realized, my fingerprints are all over that knife."

"They're not. I see to it that you'll never be incriminated." Raguel's eyes sparked. "It's just more of my *angel voodoo.* The young man with those ludicrous tattoos will—as I believe the right saying goes—take the rap."

Sharsted didn't like that idea. "But he didn't do it! I did! This is Florida; they execute people here than California lets murderers out of prison and gives them free apartments! That poor kid'll ride the lightning if he gets convicted."

Raguel popped a brow at Sharsted. "Then God's world will be better off, wouldn't you say? That tattooed dignitary didn't exactly strike me as Humanitarian of the Year. He'll have plenty of time to find God on Death Row. And how's this for a thought?" Raguel raised another emphatic finger. "You may actually have saved his soul. Like I said before, everything evens out in the end."

Sharsted pushed his glasses up. "Fantastic. Where are we going next?"

"You'll see…"

When they turned the corner, they should've seen a similar suburban street, but this was not the case. *This guy really has some tricks,* Sharsted thought, impressed. They were now strolling down a paved road lined on either side by trees, but up ahead Sharsted saw several high, bright streetlights spiring above a compound of some sort, circumscribed by ten-foot-tall chain-link fence. Within the fence stood several office trailers, and behind that was a row of parked cement trucks.

One truck was parked closer to the facility, over which stood whatever tall apparatus it was that, via conveyor belt, provided for the truck's barrel to be filled with dry cement.

One lone man, on hand-holds, stood aloft at the rear of the truck, watching as the dry concrete was conveyed into a large funnel that emptied into the barrel. The barrel was revolving, its motor noise apparent, while an attached nozzle sprayed in water.

"This," Raguel began, "is the Adamson

Cement and Paving Company, and that's Mr. Adamson there near the barrel's ingress. He's quite the entrepreneur; he started this company years ago after he'd learned the trade as a laborer. With a few thousand dollars that he'd saved, he started this business from scratch and now owns a multimillion-dollar business."

"Good for him, a captain of industry," Sharsted said. "Proof that capitalism works." But he had a bad feeling that Raguel had more to describe than Mr. Adamson's success story.

"He may look like a so-called nice guy, and certainly he's done much good for his community with regards to volunteer work and charitable donations. Ah, but that's just the *appearance,* eh? Honestly, the thoughts that man's brain generates, in my opinion, preclude him from occupying so much as a cubic inch of space on this planet. He is a pederast of the first water; the things he's done to little boys would make John Wayne Gacy look like a Cub Scout. I don't know off hand how many children he's raped and killed, but that all ends today. Thanks to you."

Guy rapes and kills little boys? Sharsted thought. *Probably tortures them too.* He nodded to himself. *I can do this…* He clapped his hands together. "Okay, so, what? You make me invisible and I go cut the dude's throat?"

"No, no, I'm afraid that would be letting Mr. Adamson off too easily," Raguel said. "I have something much better in store for the gentleman. But first, just so you know for sure…"

Raguel handed Sharsted the Lente Blasphemia; Sharsted looked.

The scene he beheld in the eyeholes was a near replication of what he'd initially seen: Adamson on the hand-holds at the back of the truck as the mixing-barrel revolved. Only now he had with him a naked one-year-old boy. The child was still alive, but barely. Adamson held it under his arm with no more difficulty than a load of laundry. The arcane optical device seemed automatically to zoom in on Adamson's face, which presented the visage of perfect evil.

Adamson calmly pushed the child into the revolving barrel. Then he peered in and down with a flashlight for a few moments, then withdrew himself, and—ever the psycho-sexual sociopath—squeezed his own crotch.

Sharsted handed back the Lente Blasphemia. "Yeah, I'm all about this one. How do you want me to do him?"

Raguel shrugged. "Just climb up there and push him in."

"And I'll be invisible?"

"Yes, you will and I will activate the Paresis

Spell so he won't be able to resist. Oh, once he's in the barrel I'll terminate the Paresis Spell; he'll instantly regain his awareness while drowning in his own cement. And wear this." Raguel opened the "tool-box," withdrew some sort of pendant with an aquamarine stone on it, and placed it around Sharsted's neck.

"What's that?"

"I won't bother telling you the actual name of this interesting artifact; just think of it as a a means of giving you a little extra *oomph*. After all, Mr. Sharsted, you're not exactly a spring chicken anymore, are you?" Raguel gave another of his witty winks.

In the space of that same wink, Sharsted felt absolutely vibrant, better than he'd felt in thirty years. "Man! That's some *oomph!*"

"Right now, Mr. Sharsted, you're stronger than several silverback gorillas. You won't know your own strength, so engage in a little self-restraint, if you will."

There was some food for thought. But for now, *time to get on with it.*

Sharsted stalked across the road and into the compound through an opened chain-link gate. AUTHORIZED PERSONEL ONLY a sign read which made him frown. *They spelled personnel wrong...* The cement truck's steady, abrasive machine-noise grew louder with each step he took closer to the truck. When he got there, Sharsted looked up at Adamson who, as promised, wasn't aware of Sharsted's arrival and wasn't moving a muscle.

Sharsted climbed right up on the hand-holds. "Hey?" he said, bumping Adamson's thigh. "Dickface? Are you really paralyzed?"

Indeed, Adamson was...

Then Sharsted side-swiped Adamson on the ladder-like hand-holds and lifted him up by the belt and—

"In ya go, dude..."

He flung the millionaire into the aperture of the mixing barrel, and that was that. After a moment, he heard garbled screaming, sloshing, and annoying high-pitched shrieks. And a few moments after that?

Nothing.

Sharsted climbed back down, not even out of breath. When he returned to Raguel, he excitedly said, "You weren't kidding about this pendant you put on me! That guy must've weighed two hundred pounds at least, but to me he felt like a sack of empty peanut shells!"

"Just another wondrous gift of God, Mr. Sharsted," Raguel replied and led them both away from the compound. "The wonders of Celestial Science! Satan and his sorcerial engineers have

EDWARD LEE

their Occult Science, we have Celestial Science, and I can tell you this: we're ahead of the game in that department." Raguel smiled. "Praise God!"

Sharsted looked at his watch. It was 8:24. *Damn, this night could last forever,* he thought.

"Time for a little fun, wouldn't you say?" Raguel said.

"Uhhhh…" Sharsted could not imagine Raguel's idea of "fun." "Sure."

"Close your eyes…"

Sharsted closed them, but it took some doing.

"Now open them."

Fuck! What's this?

Raguel's mojo, in literally the blink of an eye, had transferred them from the street where the late Mr. Adamson's cement company was to the living room of a squalid apartment. One very large African American man and one even larger Hispanic man stood aside with their preposterously muscular arms crossed. The Hispanic's t-shirt read: DUCT TAPE: IT CAN'T FIX STUPID BUT IT CAN MUFFLE THE SOUND. The black guy's t-shirt had a picture of Clint Eastwood and read WHAT ARE YOU SPOOKS UP TO? They were evidently waiting for a much smaller white man who sat on a couch leaning over a sizeable pile of drugs; he was using a popsicle stick to count off individual pills.

"Obviously a narcotics distributor," Raguel pointed out. "The two big guys are the bagmen; the scrawny white guy is the boss. And the two women are, as I believe the right term goes, the gang *bitches*."

Sharsted looked to his left and saw another beat-up couch on which two skinny nasty-looking white women sat, smoking cigarettes. Not the kind of women one would take home to meet Mom.

"You ready?" Raguel queried.

"Yeah, but… all these people were born evil?"

"Well, no." Raguel hitched his belt up against his enormous stomach. "They're all innocent, victims of negative environments and appalling childhoods."

Sharsted scratched his head. "So… what are we gonna do? Are we gonna kill them?"

Raguel looked slighted. "Of course not! But they're still bad people. We're just going to rough them up a little."

"But… why?"

"Because it's *fun* Mr. Sharsted! You need to lighten up! So don't kill them, just give them a good pranging."

"Pranging," Sharsted muttered. "Okay."

"Good. Now get ready. I'm turning off the Invisibility Totem."

Sharsted sighed, waiting. He expected some sound or feeling or pressure change but there was nothing. Suddenly, one of the couch women shouted, "Where the fuck did they come from?" Her t-shirt read I CUNT SPELL.

"Who the fuck?" yelled the skinny white guy.

"Good evening, ladies and gentlemen," Raguel announced. "Pardon the intrusion, but my colleague and I are here to formally introduce ourselves."

The big black guy with the Eastwood shirt chuckled and smacked a huge fist into his opened palm. "The fuck is this? Fat dude looks like a giant pear with a fat white head on top."

Raguel bristled. "Insults are hardly a demonstration of sophistication and good will!"

The Hispanic guy grinned, showing a cliched gold tooth. "And who deese skeeny old man look like a beggar from Caracas?"

I guess he means me, Sharsted surmised.

"Chico! Tredell!" yelled the white guy. "I want these two weirdo fucks *laid out* and *fucked over* till they tell us who they are!"

"They can't be undercover cops," said one of the girls.

"Prolee two focks from 17ᵗʰ Street Gang," speculated the Hispanic. "Trine ta scare us off our turf."

The black chuckled. "If these two cornholes

are the best they got, we'll be running this shit city soon."

Then the black guy, Tredell, and the Hispanic guy, Chico, both stepped forward with malign grins.

Sharsted's initial instincts ordered him to find safety; he stepped aside, eyeing an opened doorway to another room. But then he thought, *What am I running from? I'm stronger than both of these assholes put together!*

Tredell came forward another step. "I'll beat myself off with my hand after I work your white ass, and then Snowdrop over there will suck off your shit…"

"The hell I will!" one of the girls wailed.

Tredell lunged forward.

Some magic jazz in the pendant changed the attacker's movements to slow-motion. The big black muscular arm swung around as the giant knuckly fist went from lightning speed to a slow-as-molasses trajectory toward Sharsted's face. Sharsted merely grabbed Tredell's wrist with his left hand, the top of his forearm with his right hand, then heaved himself forward, and—

SNAP!

—broke the man's forearm against the doorframe to the next room.

Tredell collapsed with an impressive *thud!* His face webbed with deep creases from the unexpected agony, and this expression only multiplied when Sharsted stepped on his right knee and gingerly raised his right ankle until his knee folded backward. The action generated a delightful crunching sound, like someone eating kettle-cooked chips.

Tredell, bellowing, was out for the count.

But what of Raguel and *his* opponent?

"Stop being bad," Raguel suggested, then leaned over, grabbed Chico's crotch, and squeezed. Here, a different, fainter sort of crunching sound was heard, and Chico bellowed with a hair-raising intensity like that of Tredell. "You won't be impregnating any women anytime soon," Raguel assured.

Then he flicked the tip of his forefinger over his thumb, and when that forefinger made contact with Chico's jaw, his head whipped right, his jaw fractured, and most of his teeth flew out of his mouth.

Raguel looked to Sharsted with a jocular remark. "He's probably got Medicaid, don't you think?"

The rest of the forefinger's clout, then, sent Chico pin-wheeling across the room in mid-air. He slammed hard against the wall, making a man-shaped indentation into the sheet-rock, after which he flumped to the seedy floor, bloody-mouthed and unconscious.

In the meantime, Tredell, too, had lapsed into quiet unconsciousness.

"Wow!" Sharsted exclaimed. "With this pendant on, I'm like... Superman!"

"Indeed. But I suspect Superman has a higher capacity than you to maintain an awareness of his surroundings."

"What?"

"Behind you?"

Sharsted turned just in time to duck. If he *hadn't* ducked he would've been smacked in the head with by a piece of metal pipe wielded by the woman in the I CUNT SPELL t-shirt. There was no time to think; therefore Sharsted's most primitive instincts—pardon the pun—kicked in. He

FWAP!

—kicked the woman right between the legs.

"Bingo!" Raguel exclaimed.

The ragtag woman went cross-eyed, hunched over at once, clasping her groin, and tipped over onto the stain- and cigarette-butt-flecked carpet. Cheeks billowing, she glared up at Sharsted through slitted lids, and wailed, "I think you ruptured my fuckin' uterus!"

Sharsted shrugged. "Well, don't do bad things and you won't get your uterus ruptured."

She was still glowering. "What kind of a *man* kicks a woman in the pussy?"

"Listen, miss. When a *woman* is trying to hit a *man* in the head with a piece of pipe, then that *man* is entitled to kick that *woman* in the *pussy* as *hard as he can.*"

"How absolutely brutal!" Raguel approved.

Sharsted turned toward his mentor. "Um, speaking of awareness to surroundings..."

Raguel spun around just in time to face the skinny, stoop-shouldered white guy, who at that same moment discharged a bullet from at large handgun. But the slow-motion gig switched on and the bullet slowed down like some monotonous, unoriginal Marvel movie, and Raguel stepped easily out of the way. The bullet slammed into the wall, exited the wall, penetrated the neighbor's front door, flew into the neighbor's bedroom, and missed landing in the sleeping neighbor's buttocks by an inch.

Raguel took the gun away from white guy and bent it into a curious U-shape. "Shame on you for sneaking up on me like that!" Then he slapped white guy on the back, the kinetic energy of which caused both of the white guy's eyeballs to start from their sockets, after which they dangled from raw nerves like two ping pong balls on strings. He flipped across the couch, out cold.

"Damn, man," Sharsted objected. "Isn't that

overdoing it a little? I mean, you popped his *eyeballs* out."

"No worries. The EMTs will probably be able to put them back in. And look who's talking—you just ruptured that woman's *uterus*." Raguel leaned back and let out a hearty laugh. "No more food-card babies for her!"

"Whatever," Sharsted muttered.

"But you're not done yet, Mr. Sharsted. There's still one more miscreant to go, is there not?" Raguel pointed to the corner of the room.

There, shivering, and her teeth actually *chattering,* stood the second scrawny prostitute. This one's t-shit read I SHOULD'VE BEEN SWALLOWED. Teary-eyed, she held her hands up in a hopeless plea. "Please, don't kill me, I beg you. I'll do anything…"

"Your call, Mr. Sharsted. Do you want to rupture *her* uterus as well? Let's see what you're really made of, shall we?"

Sharsted faced the terrified prostitute. "All right, here's how it's gonna be. No more taking drugs and no more selling drugs, okay? No more prostituting yourself, and no more hanging out with pieces of shit like these guys? Got it?"

The woman's teeth were still chattering. "I guh-guh-guh-guh-got it!"

"If you do any of that stuff ever again, I

will know, and then I will muss your hair like it's never been mussed." He pointed down to I CUNT SPELL. "If you think *she* got it bad, you don't know what bad is. Got it?"

"I guh-guh–!"

"Now get out of here."

"Thuh-thuh-thank you!" The petrified woman fled the apartment as fast as just about any human pair of feet could take her.

"Well done, Mr. Sharsted!" Raguel belted out. "I am truly impressed!"

"Well, forgiveness and all that, right?"

"Right! Just as God so loved the world!"

Sharsted rubbed his eyes. "God, yes. I mean, look at this." He indicated all four unconscious reprobate scumbags in the room. "We really fucked these people up, but you said they weren't born evil, right?"

"That is indeed correct."

"So you're telling me that all this mayhem is cool with God?"

"Oh, I don't know, but I do know this: God grants to his soldiers—that's you and me, for example—some discretionary freedoms. So don't worry about it. We did a lot of good tonight."

"Yeah, I—" He winced at the white guy with his eyes popped out. "I guess we did. What's next on the agenda?"

"You want to see some *real* angel voodoo?"

"Yeah, this is starting to get interesting."

Raguel pointed to the veritable *pile* of opioids on the table. He raised a hand over the pile and closed his eyes. At once, the pills all levitated off the table then floated down the hall. A moment later, a toilet was heard flushing.

Sharsted was wide-eyed. "Wow. That rocks! Can I do that?"

"In time, Mr. Sharsted. More powers will be granted to you as you continue to succeed in your probationary period. And of course, God understands that time and effort is worth money so…" Raguel picked up several bands of hundred-dollar bills off the table. "God considers ill-gotten gains confiscated during good works to be fully appropriate."

Astonished, Sharsted took the bands of bills. *Cool! Looks like I'm getting that 84-inch TV after all. I guess God's a capitalist!*

"Time for us to go, Mr. Sharsted."

Sirens could be heard in the distance. They exited the shitty apartment, turned, and—

Just keeps getting nuttier and nuttier, Sharsted thought to himself.

"This will be a grim one, Mr. Sharsted," said Raguel. He was leading Sharsted down a long straight dark road with no vehicles in sight. Dense sonic sheets of cricket chirrups and cicada drones throbbed in the air. Trees lined either side of the road.

"Where are we going now?"

"Due time, my friend," Raguel said, "But tell me this. Wasn't it gratifying back there?"

"What? Beating the shit out of those druggers?" Sharsted considered the question. "Yeah. Those guys are a plague to their own impoverished neighborhoods. Those drugs they sell kill people at an epidemic proportion. They sell drugs to *kids*. They ruin lives for profit. Pieces of shit like that should be executed. Come to think of it..." Sharsted looked to Raguel. "Why didn't we just kill them?"

"I told you, they weren't born evil, Mr. Sharsted. They're no less victims than the people they sell their wares to."

Sharsted didn't know if he bought that. "Okay, fine."

Raguel chuckled. "But I'm more interested in your *base* reaction. That woman, the one with the vulgar t-shit. She's a victim too, you know. Her childhood beggars description." He held up a finger. "But still. Wasn't it *relieving*, I mean, didn't it grant to you an extraordinary sense of *satisfaction*, just to haul back and kick that ninety-pound prostitute right in the vagina?"

Sharsted scowled, started to answer, "No! Of course n–" but them floundered.

Raguel grinned. "Come on, admit it, Mr. Sharsted. In actuality it was *fun,* wasn't it?"

"I, uhhhh…"

"Don't deceive yourself for false appearances. It's okay. It's perfectly natural to release your most primitive instincts when the occasion calls for it, don't you think?"

Sharsted couldn't answer, but he almost grinned when he remembered that deep fat FWAP! sound when his foot socked up between her legs. "All right, you've got me. I admit it. Kicking that hosebag in the pussy so hard her uterus broke was *fun.* In fact, it might've been the most fun I've *ever* had."

"Good, good! Honesty means more than anything!"

They walked a bit farther in the moon-tinseled darkness, amid the swelling chorus of crickets and periodic caws of nightbirds.

"Here we are," Raguel said. He'd stopped on the road's shoulder and extended a hand across the street to a small clearing which was attached to a path leading into the woods. Sharsted thought he could smell a marsh; he heard distant splashing sounds as of fish jumping out of water.

"Here comes our gentleman," Raguel confirmed.

Two headlights appeared down the road. Raguel pulled Sharsted back behind some trees. Eventually a dented van slowed down and backed into the clearing.

Raguel glared. "Abominable, absolutely abominable…"

Sharsted looked on.

A man got out of the van, a typical ragtag Florida redneck. Did Sharsted hear the muffled sounds of dog barking?

The redneck opened the back of the van and began shooing out–

"No," Sharsted muttered when he noted the redneck's t-shirt, which read PUPPIES R US!

"This pride and joy of humanity," Raguel began, "co-owns what is known as a puppy mill. They breed dogs in deplorable conditions and sell the puppies to pet shops. But of course, due to much forced inbreeding, a good number of the puppies are born sick and with defects; they can't be sold, So it's this humanitarian's job to dispense with them as cheaply as possible."

Sharsted was steaming inside; he could feel his face turning red as he watched the redneck throwing puppies out of the back of the van. There was one puppy with a tumor on its back, and other with a colossal eye infection. And here was another with some catastrophic outbreak of mange that left a great swath of its back hairless. And yet another puppy with only three legs.

"So the motherfucker just abandons the

puppies in the woods where they'll starve to death."

"Not just *any* woods, Mr. Sharsted, and they seldom live long enough to starve to death." Raguel pointed behind them down the road.

Sharsted couldn't help but see the sign: EVERGLADES STATE PARK—DO NOT FEED OR APPROACH THE ALLIGATORS.

Sharsted could've throw up. "I'm taking him out..."

"Wait, wait. You haven't yet witnessed the entirety of the story." Raguel gave Sharsted the Lente Blasphemia. "Look in the device, Mr. Sharsted, and see what this esquire will do several years from now..."

Sharsted watched the same redneck getting out of the same van in the exact same place. The redneck was a little fatter now—Sharsted presumed the puppy business was good—and he now had one of those Metallica mustaches.

"Murder for hire, Mr. Sharsted," informed Raguel. "But the main reason he does it isn't for the money, it's simply because he's evil. It gives him a thrill, a *sexual* thrill..."

In this future glimpse, Sharsted felt like a gallon of ice water had emptied into his stomach. He watched the redneck pull not puppies but two squalling human babies out of the van, grinning maleficently, and then carry them upside down by the ankles, like potato sacks, down the same path toward the marsh, or whatever body of water existed down there.

Next came something like a jump-cut in a movie. A small lake glimmered before him in the moonlight. But out in that lake, several sets of orange eyes watched the activity on the shore. The redneck dropped both babies, then shouted, "Soup's on!" The babies squirmed, wailing, in the mud. When the redneck turned away and went back to the van, four alligators slowly approached the spot where two very tender meals awaited.

The future snapped off as Sharsted handed the Lente Blasphemia back to Raguel. "This guy's ass is grass. Make it so I'm not invisible, okay?"

"Very well..."

Sharsted stalked across the street. The redneck had corralled the puppies away from the street and down the trail. The barking had lessened considerably, and that wasn't a good sign.

"What do you want?" the redneck demanded when he noticed Sharsted.

FWAP!

Sharsted kicked the redneck right between the legs. The redneck went bug-eyed and fell over. All he could do in response was gasp, clutching his crotch.

"No more doggie killing for you, asshole. And you won't be killing any babies either—thanks to *me."*—

Sharsted grabbed the man by his throat and dragged him, choking and gurgling, down the trail. But his heart sank when he got to the shore. There were no longer any puppies in evidence, just a few puppy *parts,* like legs and tails, and even one little boxer's head. Several alligators slid into the water; their bellies looked pretty full.

"You scumbag! You pile of garbage!" Sharsted yelled. He wanted to step on the guy's head and crack it open like a coconut, but… *That's too good for him.*

He wasn't consciously considering Raguel's previous remarks about baser and more primitive instincts; nevertheless, he yanked down the redneck's pants and instantly grabbed his cock and balls by the root and ripped them out of his groin. Then he flung the severed genitals into the water, where the fleshy mass was swallowed whole by a roving gator.

Of course, that peaceful, still, quiet night was quickly interrupted by the redneck's heaving caterwauls of agony, but more agony would follow when—

CRACK!

—Sharsted folded the man in half, backwards, and severed his spine, leaving him to quiver paralyzed in the mud.

He yelled out to the lake, "Soup's on!" just as several more gators cruised toward the shoreline, eyeing the new prey soaked in aromatic fresh blood.

"Fuck this shit, man!" Sharsted complained when he got back to the road. "All those puppies got eaten."

"The world is a sad affair, I'm afraid, since Lucifer and his confederates established themselves. But at least you can find some solace in knowing that that despicable redneck will be eaten as well. And more solace, too, in the assurance that no babies will ever share a similar fate."

Sharsted sputtered. It was no solace. It sucked. *This world's a piece of shit. How can anyone feed puppies to gators?*

"Yes, Mr. Sharsted. The world seems like a horrible place but sometimes—*sometimes*—it really is beautiful if you look hard enough."

"Great. So who's the next devil-worshiping scumbag I kill? I can't fuckin' wait."

As they walked, the road and the trees on either side seemed to lapse-dissolve into nothing but bright-white stars like luminous spillage in the sky. That's all Sharsted could see anywhere he looked, even down; it was as though he and Raguel were walking weightlessly through infinite heavens.

So there really is a God, Sharsted admitted to himself. *And He really did create everything, all of this, from every star in the universe to every microorganism in the sea to every molecule everywhere.*

How could he not believe that now after all he'd witnessed just in the last twenty-four hours?

Light seemed to emit from Raguel's eyes. "Yes, such a beautiful place, a paradise, in fact, full of wonder and joy, full of bunnies, blooming flowers, chirping birds, snow-scaped mountains, lush green pastures, awesome waterfalls, indescribable sunrises—all that, and then we have Satan and his accomplices who only exist to ruin it all. Why do they want to ruin it? Because God made it all for His flock, and Satan can't stand that. He was so humiliated and enraged when God evicted him from Heaven that he will devote thousands of years to besmirching all things beautiful."

"Yeah," Sharsted said, still bristling from the puppy incident. "*Fuck* Satan, and *bugger* anyone on his side, I'd like to toss 'em all in a wood chipper and take a shower in their blood and guts."

Raguel popped his eyebrows. "That's quite a stalwart level of devotion, Mr, Sharsted, but I must say... the visual is a bit unsettling."

"Unsettling?" Sharsted chuckled. "You just made me slash a teenage babysitter's throat, but *I'm* unsettling?"

"Well, I didn't *make* you. You elected to do so of your own free will, all in the service of opposing evil and celebrating all that is good."

"Fine." Sharsted remained content, as insane as that might've seemed. He knew that he'd slit the throats of a thousand evil teenaged babysitters if it would make the world even just a tiny bit better. "I'm kind of chomping at the bit here, Raguel," he admitted. "What's next on the agenda?"

Even as the words were leaving Sharsted's mouth, their stunning ramble through the depths of space prolapsed and reformed...

He now stood on the balcony of a high-rise condo. Where, exactly, he didn't know, but it occurred to him now that that hardly mattered. He looked out of a dizzying cityscape of flickering lights and thoroughfares beating like lit arteries amid the entire urban purlieu.

"Let's go in," Raguel suggested, and opened the sliding-glass door.

A plethora of luxury greeted them when they entered: a spacious room adorned by plush, dark carpeting, high-end furniture, and what could only be a millionaire's entertainment center. *Must be nice,* Sharsted thought.

"The owner of this luxurious abode is a gentleman by the name of Cornelius Van Houter. He hides his astronomical earnings by third-world forced-labor enterprises behind a mire of counterfeit charitable institutions and phony hedge-funding." Raguel's expression and demeanor went blank in a sudden solemnity. "Honestly, things that this man has done are wholly impossible to retail; they make me want to fall to my knees and cry like a baby."

Sharsted felt alarmed. "Wow, it must be *really* bad."

"Oh, it is, I assure you, it is…" Raguel reeled his hand forward in a "right this way" gesture. "Back here."

They walked into a master bedroom bigger than the entirety of Sharsted's domicile. One corner was occupied by a commodious hot-tub, and in that tub two people lounged, with glasses of wine at their sides. One was an attractive woman—

"She's a call-girl, one of his favorites," Raguel revealed. "Harmless really. And there—"

Also in the tub sat a tanned, debonaire fiftyish man with intense eyes and stylish gray temples.

"– is your assignment, the venerable Monsieur Van Houter. Looks like nothing more than a serious businessman, does he not? But he's also a serious Satanist."

"Really? You mean he, like, dresses up in a hooded black cloak and prays in front of a altar of black candles with a pentagram and all that?"

"All that and more, Mr. Sharsted. It may seem

quite hackneyed to you, but Van Houter and his kind are *steadfast* in their devotion to their master, for it is *to* that master that he owes his riches and power."

Sharsted shrugged. "Hate to say it, but he just looks like a primped older guy sitting in a hot tub with a hot chick. I can't see him doing that whole Lucifer gig in the silly get-ups and people wearing Party City horns."

Raguel smiled close-mouthed and handed Sharsted the Lente Blasphemia.

When Sharsted looked, he saw a mock Black Mass, like something in a cheesy movie: a grotto lit by flickering black candles and a stone altar erected before a half-circle of nincompoops in black cloaks and hoods. From each participant's neck dangled necklaces sporting pentagrams, planetary symbols, sigils and, of course, most cliched of all, inverted crosses.

"This will take place on Roodmas Eve, three nights from now," Raguel said.

Sharsted felt confounded. *Roodmas, schmoodmas. Doesn't look like there's anything worth killing Van Houter for. He just playing Halloween with a bunch of silly butt-munchers.* "Watch," Raguel said.

One figure departed from the rest and lowered his hood. It was Van Houter. The man raised his hands in some pompous gesture, then nodded, and—

Sharsted jolted in place.

Just before the altar, from the ceiling, dropped six newborn babies of all colors. The tiny things churned in mid-air, puff-faced, unable to make any noise. Why no noise?

Because they were being hanged by their necks with piano wire.

"Van Houter buys the babies in the city ghettos," Raguel informed. "What more perfect distillation of evil can there be than producing drugs so potent that addict mothers will sell their babies as sacrifice-fodder for endeavors such as this?"

Sharsted gulped, staring at the iniquitous spectacle. One by one, the babies' struggles ceased, leaving them to hang limp. Pristine blood ran down their tiny bodies, down their legs, and dripped off their minuscule feet to *plip plip plip* into bowls arranged on the floor.

"And he's done this countless times in the past," Raguel went on. "But now? 'Vengeance is Mine, saith the Lord.'"

Sharsted shoved the Lente Blasphemia away, mortified. "Let me strangle *him* with piano wire. I'll do it real slow…"

"No, I think you'll find this apparatus much more gratifying." Raguel opened his "tool-box" and removed a single tiny pebble which looked yellowish. "This is genuine brimstone, Mr.

Sharsted, and not just any old piece of sulphur but sulphur from Hell. It's *very difficult* for those of us on God's side of the fence to procure. But here it is, after much travail." He placed the pebble into Sharsted's palm.

"What do I do with it?"

Raguel winked. "Just toss it into the hot tub when I tell you to, but first, I've gotta get her out of there. She's innocent."

With a quizzical stare, Sharsted watched his mentor approach the hot tub. By now, Van Houter and his mistress were paralyzed and unaware of anything. Raguel began to haul the woman out of the tub by a handful of her shiny wheat-blond hair.

"Really? By the *hair?*" Sharsted exclaimed, jolted. "That's pretty abusive to someone who's innocent, isn't it?"

Raguel looked up and smiled joyously. "Abusive?" Now the nude woman lay half out of the tub, her hips inclined upward. Sharsted had no choice but to notice that her pubic region sported a *bounteous* plot of blond hair.

"How's *this* for abusive?" Raguel went on. Now he grabbed a handful of the woman's *pubic hair* and hauled her the rest of the way out of the tub.

Sharsted winced. "I didn't know angels could be so misogynistic..."

Raguel released his grasp; the woman's body

slapped wetly to the tiled floor. "Misogynistic? And that from the upstanding luminary who, not very long ago, kicked a woman—your word, not mine—in the *pussy*. Oh, for goodness' sake, Mr. Sharsted. Relax. Believe me, this dizzy trollop can't feel a thing." He paused for effect. "Now, please toss that pebble into the hot tub where Mr. Van Houter is enjoying his final moments of life. I will take off the Paresis Spell immediately."

Sharsted was unable to imagine what to expect. He took a breath, let it out, and tossed the pebble into the hot-tub.

… plip…

In the time it takes for someone to snap their fingers once, the water in the hot tub was boiling furiously. Steam in a great white cloud billowed upward, so hot that Sharsted had to lurch away. Mr. Van Houter's screams sounded so loud that it seemed as if his inmost soul were being yanked out of him. The man was lobster-red in seconds and swelling from head-to-toe, blistered. Maniacal convulsions turned him into a bobbing, shrieking buoy of agony. His irises turned opaque white like a hard-boiled egg. Propelled by the torments of the damned, Van Houter shuddered as he made to crawl out of the tub.

"He's crawling out!" Sharsted exclaimed.

"And what do we do when they crawl out, Mr.

Sharsted?" Raguel winked once more. "Why, we *push them back in!*"

Sharsted didn't feel too great about the prospect, but then his assessment changed when he remembered the six newborn babes hanging by piano wire. He raised his right foot, applied the bottom of his Walmart velcro sneaker to the top of Van Houter's steaming head, shoved, and—

SPLASH!

—back into the churning water he went. Moments later, the millionaire was doing a Dead Man's Float in the furiously roiling water. The entire top of his head was a wet, hair-covered blister.

In the space of another finger-snap, the water stopped boiling; in fact, the heat from the turbulence could no longer be felt.

"I'd say Mr. Van Houter is done," Raguel said, rubbing his hands together.

The remnant redolence reminded Sharsted of his dear grandmother's chicken noodle soup.

Raguel pointed to the middle of the tub. "Now I'm afraid I'll have to ask you to retrieve the pebble, but you needn't worry, the water is now room temperature."

Sharsted hesitated, but then shrugged. *He hasn't bullshitted me yet.* Grimacing, he stepped down into the tepid, protein-enriched soup that had been the water and waded past Van

Houter's floating body. A side-glance provided an ideal angle to see that the previous super-hot temperature had ejected the corpse's intestines out through its mouth. They floated palely like enormous udon noodles.

Worse than that, some disproportion of buoyancy had occurred—perimortal gasses, perhaps—and this caused Van Houter's corpse to turn over in the water, belly-side up. Sharsted's awareness thankfully would not allow him to look at the decedent's face but by happenstance, he did catch an unwilling glimpse of the man's scrotum—

Aw, fuck off! Sharsted thought. *Look at his nut-sack!*

—which had by now ballooned to something the size of a volleyball, but, alas, this was a *maroon* volleyball. So strong the water's heat had been that it flooded Van Houter's "nut-sack" with blood. And then the blood had boiled to a semi-solid puree.

It was then Sharsted vomited mightily into the water. Dizzy, he reached down, claimed the pebble and jumped back out.

"Thank you," Raguel said. He placed the pebble back in the "toolbox." "This can only be used every seventy-seven days—it needs time to recharge."

"How-how big a pool can that thing bring to a boil?"

Raguel smiled. "Do you *really* want to know, Mr. Sharsted?"

"Well, yeah, I think so. Like a community-type swimming pool?"

Raguel, still smiling, shook his head. "Bigger."

"Like, maybe, an Olympic-sized pool?"

"No, Mr. Sharsted. You're thinking too small. Try Lake Superior. And if you want to see some *real* climate change, drop this little doozy into the Arctic ocean and see what happens."

Note to self, Sharsted thought. *DON'T do that.*

Raguel nodded with approval at Van Houter's scarlet corpse. "I'm happy to say that our friend here will be *missing* his little Roodmas Eve party."

"Yeah, but wait a minute," Sharsted observed. "There were other Satanists there too. How do you know they won't still hang those babies with piano wire?"

Raguel looked at his watch, revealing that it was a Mickey Mouse watch. "You can rest assured that by now, Mr. Van Houter's cronies have all been— as I believe the right saying goes—taken out."

"By who?"

"*Whom.* By other subcontractors."

This sparked Sharsted's curiosity. "Oh, so I'm not the only one."

"Far from it Mr. Sharsted. The instant the Celestial Congress got the go-ahead via the new law, every Caliginaut in Heaven was dispatched to Earth to recruit subcontractors. What was that great old Jerry Lee Lewis song? There's gonna be a whole lotta slaughterin' goin' on!" Raguel, then, looked this way and that, recomposed himself, patted his chest, and said, "Time for us to go, but before we leave, I need you to drag our poor call-girl out to the balcony and throw her over the rail."

Sharsted reacted as if struck in the head. "What! No! I'm not doing that!" He looked down at the attractive, blond, and very inert young woman with the veritable *pile* of butterscotch pubic hair. "It's not right! She's harmless! She doesn't deserve to die!"

Raguel released a long sigh. "Gracious, Mr. Sharsted. I'm *kidding*. Really, has all the mirth been drained out of this desolate world? Let's move on to our next gallivant." He looked at Sharsted intensely. "It will be our last of the evening, after which I will—as I believe the right saying goes—*cut you loose* to your new divine duties…"

Sharsted followed Raguel out of Van Houter's big bedroom, turned, and immediately found himself in a brightly lit and very sterile and tile-floored hallway where Raguel stood bent over, his huge belly depending, as he repeatedly yanked the handle of a vending machine. Then, from the machine, he collected up no less than *seven* Kit-Kat bars.

"Really?" Sharsted asked, cruxed. "You're gong to eat *seven* Kit-Kats?"

Raguel scowled up as if abraded by a scathing defamation. "Well, Mr. Sharsted, I happen to be hungry and these Kit-Kat bars are quite the satisfier."

"Yeah, sure, but… *seven?*"

"Seven is the Holy Number, while six proves the number of error—Lucifer's number. It's the number of eternal darkness. Seven is the number of eternal light."

We're talking about fuckin' candy bars! Sharsted grumbled to himself. "Did you even pay for them?"

"Of course not—"

"So you stole them. Is that the example an angel should be setting?"

Raguel's fat lips puckered. "God created this world for *you,* for *humans.* And since I serve *your* creator, that means *I* can help myself to anything that God has provided for you. Is that reasonable, Mr. Sharsted?'

"Lemme get this right. *God* said it's okay for you to steal Kit-Kat bars?"

"Yes, Mr. Sharsted, He did. He also said it's okay for me to exterminate any human I so desire. If a human gets on my nerves, then I can wipe that person from the face of this pretty planet. Am I succeeding in securing your attention?"

Sharsted piped down fast. "Oh, yes, yes. I was just theorizing. Didn't mean to get on your nerves."

"Good." Raguel began eating his Kit-Kats two at a time. They were gone in a minute.

What a glutton…

"I heard that, Mr.. Sharsted."

For shit's sake! "No, I said, I'm a *glutton* for punishment."

"Um-hmm."

"So where are we now?" Down the hall he saw what appeared to be a nurse's station. "Is this a hospital?"

"Yes, it is, and we have an urgent appointment right around this corner…"

As they walked, they passed several doctors with proverbial stethoscopes, several nurses, a janitor rolling a bucket to its next onus, and an orderly rushing down the hall pushing an wizened old man on a gurney. Raguel's Invisibility Totem continued to work like a charm, pun intended.

After another ten or so yards, they stopped at another nurse's station. *Mama mia,* Sharsted thought when eyeing several nurses. They stood clustered around the front desk, yapping and showing each other pictures on their phones. There were three of them, and their existence as they were demonstrated a veritable trifecta of 21st Century Female Desirability.

Damn! Sharsted thought, noting a growing pressure in his pants. *Tits, butts, hour-glass bods, and screaming cameltoes. What I wouldn't give…*

"Stop lusting after those nurses," Raguel admonished. "They're not pieces of meat to provide you with masturbation fuel. They're creations of *God,* and it's obscene and ill-mannered for you to project your rampant lust upon them. You're offending your friendship with the Lord."

Creations of God, fine. But I'll bet those girls have sucked more dick than Stormy Daniels. "Yeah, sure, but take a look at the set of—"

"This is *serious,* Mr. Sharsted. Please, hear me well." Raguel unknowingly sported a smudge of Kit-Kat chocolate at the corner of his mouth, which completely usurped his efforts to enforce the gravity of the situation. "Have you ever heard of a Whiskey 79 warhead?"

This heightened Sharsted's attention. "No, but… it doesn't sound good."

A tiny *click* was heard as Raguel made some minute adjustment on the Lente Blasphemia. "Have a butcher at that, as I believe the British say."

"What? A butch—"

"Just look in the eyeholes!"

Sharsted looked in the eyeholes and saw a razor-sharp image of what appeared to be an artillery shell standing on end. The shell was painted flat olive-drab and had a white band toward the top and a shiny black tip. When Sharsted narrowed his eyes, the image zoomed to some stenciled writing on the side of the shell that very clearly read PROPERTY OF U.S. ARMY MUNITIONS COMMAND—ONE (1) W79 AFAP—YIELD, SELECTABLE 1.1-100 KT—FUZE M735—SELECTABLE.

"Uh," Sharsted uttered. "I'm not liking what I'm seeing…"

Finally, Raguel wiped off the chocolate smudge and licked it off his finger. "It's an obsolete nuclear artillery shell, Mr. Sharsted. Over 500 were manufactured and warehoused for years, but in the early nineties they were dismantled in Texas as part of a disarmament accord. Of course, you'll not be surprised to learn that your treacherous government built many more, better such munitions in secret. Be that as it may, and as I've said, roughly 500 were dismantled, but one, I'm afraid, was cleverly absconded with by an enterprise that wishes to do as much harm as possible—"

"Terrorists," Sharsted supposed.

"No, worse. *Satanists.* Thirty-four years from now, the stolen warhead will be detonated in the closet of an office supply store quite near the White House. The Red Chinese will be blamed." One of Raguel's eyebrows popped up, quite like Mr. Spock. "Can you hazard a guess as to what will take place next?"

Sharsted's lower lip trembled. "Uh... World War Three?"

"Yes, Mr. Sharsted. World War Three. Tens of millions will die. Whole cities will be destroyed. Whole cultures will be essentially eradicated. All because of one person, one servitor to Lucifer."

"So I have to kill the guy before he pulls this off," Sharsted reckoned.

"Yes."

Sharsted nodded. "Okay. Easy peasy. Lemme at him."

It was here that Raguel displayed a smile that seemed wholly nefarious. "Your enthusiasm is commendable. Follow me, he's in here."

Sharsted's gut plummeted when he noticed the sign on the glass door they were about to pass though.

MATERNITY WARD.

Oh, fuck. Not another baby...

There were at least twenty little maternity cribs arranged about the room, and each one occupied by its own chubby little bundle of diaper-wrapped joy.

Sharsted looked down at all those cute little faces. *And I have to kill one of them. Can I really do this?*

"Nothing is easy, Mr. Sharsted. If you don't believe me, ask Job, ask Daniel, ask St. Ignatius. The latter was sentenced to be torn limb from limb by starving dogs for praising Jesus and refusing to bow down to the ridiculous Roman gods. But the Romans gave him a choice. 'Denounce Jesus, and you will be pardoned. You may walk free.' St. Ignatius said no. And he was thrown to the dogs with a smile on his face. Now *that* is hard to do, even harder than what's being asked of you."

Sharsted gulped. He was sweating, shivering. "Okay. Which one?"

"Ah but if things were only that easy," Raguel said. He waved down at one of the babies; the baby belched. "We think of God as *omniscient,* One who knows all things. But that's only fundamentally true when you rake through the minutiae. After all, why would God send His Only Son to enable the salvation to all of mankind, if He already knew in advance who will be saved and who will not?"

Sharsted was starting to smell a rat. "What are you saying?"

Raguel cleared his throat. "What I'm saying,

Mr. Sharsted, is this: we know that one of the babies in this room will perpetrate the most devastating war in all of human history. But…" And there he went, raising that proverbial fat finger again. "We don't know precisely *which* baby it is."

Sharsted, his lower lip sticking out, stared blankly at Raguel. "And?"

"And *that* means, Mr. Sharsted, and I'm very sorry to be the bearer of this disconsolate news, you will have to kill *every baby in this maternity ward.*"

"Fuck you!" Sharsted exploded. "That's outrageous!"

"It may be, but it is also your divine assignment. There's nothing I can do."

"I'm *not* murdering a room full of babies just because you incompetent *idiots* don't know the right one!"

Raguel looked back sternly. "It's God's will."

"If killing all these babies is God's will, then God's a *dick,* and He's an *asshole! And* so are you!"

Raguel smiled, head down cast, rubbing the bridge of his eyes. "Got'cha again, Mr. Sharsted. Of course, I'm only kidding–"

Sharsted almost collapsed. "Cut that shit out, man! What are you, in junior high? It's not funny!"

"Oh, it's immensely funny, and that's why God gave us a sense of humor. How dull life would be without it, hmm?"

Sharsted was shaking his head, grinding his teeth. "Kiss my motherfuckin' ass!"

Raguel chuckled so steadily that his cheeks turned pink. "Your reaction is worth all the gold in the vaults of King Croesus. You need to *chill,* as I believe the right term goes."

Sharsted wanted to kick Raguel in the balls but... thought the better of it.

"No, Mr. Sharsted, you will only be expected to kill *one* baby in this room." Raguel set his hand down on the edge of a crib. "*This* baby."

Sharsted looked at the baby. It was swathed in a blanket populated with smiling elephants and turtles, and it grinned gleefully up at Sharsted. "You gotta be shitting me! It's the cutest little baby in the whole fuckin' place!"

"Indeed! He likes you, Mr. Sharsted. He thinks you're his daddy!"

"Yeah, well fuck that noise."

"And how ironic, hmm? You're actually *not* his daddy. You're his executioner. You're the Shadow of Death."

What am I doing? How did I even get involved with this fat whack-job? A label on the crib read FORBES, BENTLEY with a sting of numbers behind it. *Bentley. Am I really gonna KILL Bentley?* He stared longer at the baby, who was now making spit-bubbles as he grinned back up to Sharsted.

"I... I don't think I can do it," he admitted.

"Come now, Mr. Sharsted. It won't be the first baby you've murdered tonight."

"Yeah, but I didn't have to *look* at that baby. It was in the redneck chick's stomach." He looked again. "No. I don't think I can do it."

"Well then let me ask you this very hackneyed question. If you knew what would follow, could you bring yourself to exterminate Adolf Hitler as a newborn child?"

"Yeah. But this is different."

"How is it different? The only difference is that *this* baby, little Bentley, will kill far more people than Hitler did, and cause much, much more destruction, hardship, and horror."

"I don't know why it's different, it just is!"

"Stop beating around the bush, as I believe the right saying goes," Raguel urged. "Just wrap your hands around this cutie-pie's neck and *strangle* the little bugger. If you don't, he will bring ruination upon the world and all its people. It will be *apocalyptic*."

Raguel's words kept clanging hard in Sharsted's head. *Ruination,* he thought. *Tens of millions dead...* Sharsted took a jittery breath, began to lower his shaking hands, but then—

"So... I have to do this kind of stuff for the rest of my life?"

"Yes."

"But you can't tell me how long I will live."

"Well, I *can,* but I don't think it's a good idea."

"Why?"

"Because your agreement is an exhibition of faith. It doesn't matter when you will die."

Sharsted's head churned over the words. "But you *could* tell me when I'll die if you wanted to?"

Raguel huffed out a sign. "Yes. But it doesn't matter."

"It matters to me! Tell me when I'm gonna die so I know how long I'll have to do this!"

Raguel smirked. "Very well, Mr. Sharsted. This is against my better judgment but… you will die on the Ides of March at the age of seventy-nine."

Seventy-nine! That's fifteen years from now! I've still got plenty of life!

"And don't misunderstand me, Mr. Sharsted. You won't have to exterminate the hellborn every day. Just every now and then, and very few of them will be babies. It's really a terrific circumstance, since you'll be protected from all harm at all times." Raguel pointed to Sharsted's pendant. "And you'll be endowed with impressive preternatural powers. Not to mention that you are allowed to keep all money and valuables that you procure from the hellborn. You'll be *fabulously* wealthy."

Oh, man. This is sounding better and better.

Raguel continued, with a smile. "You'll be able to move out of that roach-motel apartment of yours and relocate anywhere. You can live in a luxury condo in the upper west side of Manhattan if you so desire. *And—*" There went up another emphatic finger, "– your salvation is guaranteed. No stopping off first in Purgatory. You'll be delivered straight to Heaven at the instant of your decease. It's God's reward to you for being a reasonable moralistic, decent, compassionate person for the whole of your life. Very few people are granted such an opportunity."

That was that. Sharsted cracked his knuckles. *Okay. Let's do this*

He tried not to look at little Brentley's face but some cruel synapse in his brain *forced* him to. He lowered and gently wrapped his hands around the baby's throat. The throat felt tiny. He could feel veins pulsing in it.

"One, two, three, *squeeze*, Mr. Sharsted, and it will all be over, Squeeze hard and you'll disconnect the baby's head from his spine. Death will be instantaneous and wholly absent of pain."

Sharsted's teeth chattered. *One, two, three, squeeze, one, two, three, squeeze,* he kept telling himself over and over. But…

But the commands of his brain refused to travel to his hands. He looked once more at little Brentley. The baby grinned up resplendently at him and said, "Goo! Gaa!"

Sharsted stepped back, addressed his gaze to Raguel's eyes, and said, "Sorry. I can't do it. Fire me. I want out."

"Take a moment to recompose yourself, Mr. Sharsted. Give yourself time to reflect on the grievousness of the matter and summon the proper verve and attitude."

"Nope." In Sharsted's mind, it was settled. "I can't do it, and I won't do it. You've got the wrong guy. I'm not the man for the job."

Raguel's stern expression trebled in intensity. "Are you sure?"

"Yeah."

Raguel paused, stone-faced. "I'll ask once more. Are you sure? Are you absolutely certain that you want to terminate our agreement? There will be no second chances."

"It's evil," Sharsted intoned.

"I couldn't agree more," Raguel said. "This baby *is* evil. It is the very *incarnation* of evil, and a precursor for the Anti-Christ. Don't allow yourself to be deceived. It is part of Lucifer's machinations to hide his true goals in camouflage such as this." Raguel opened his hand to indicate the adorable little baby. "Be the stalwart Christian soldier. Save the world."

A deep deep breath now, and then he thought, *One more time.* Sharsted placed his hands on the baby's throat, closed his eyes, and *squeezed.*

The baby began to choke; its heart-rate jumped, the sudden increase of which Sharsted felt in his fingers. Harder, harder…

The action shoveled images into his head like coal into a furnace. Amid a glittering black veil, Sharsted watch SS soldiers toss babies back and forth, catching them on bayonets, each soldier guttering black laughter.

Then, before a great stone bull-headed effigy, Carthaginian priests dropped live babes one after another all day long into a deep-dug trench which roared with a high-reaching wood fire.

Then he espied a massive dumpster a hundred feet long, ten high and twenty deep, full off countless squalling naked babies, hundreds and hundreds of them while a man darkened by obsidian shadows looked down from a windowed station and pushed a button; the dumpster wasn't a dumpster, it was an industrial trash compactor and as its walls collapsed in the midst of a great machine noise, the compactor's living contents was slowly squashed to human porridge, and the sound of all those dying babies reached down and down and down like a gorgeous melody, soliciting a smile from Satan himself, and the man in the station who'd pushed the button was Sharsted.

Sharsted released the baby's throat. "Nope. I refuse to do it."

Raguel looked back forlornly and slumped. "So be it."

"Yeah." *Fuck, I need a beer...*

Raguel raised his hand and by some turn of his angelic "mojo," the pendant rose off of Sharsted's neck, then floated through mid-air to land in Raguel's hand. "You won't be needing this anymore."

"No, I sure won't. Give it to the next guy."

Raguel stowed the implement back into his "tool-box." "It's a shame, Mr. Sharsted. I was beginning to like you, That's not something I've experienced much with humans."

"I was beginning to like you too." Sharsted shook his head. "But I can't kill babies."

"So you've said. Good luck to you, Mr. Sharsted."

"You too." Sharsted walked out of the maternity ward, feeling as relieved as if all the weight of the pyramids of Giza had been lifted off his shoulders.

Before the door closed behind him, he took one long look back over his shoulder, and saw

Raguel bent over little Bentley's crib and lowering his hands into it. He heard tiny gargling sounds just as the door fully closed.

"Oh, well. What a night, huh?" he asked himself and started walking.

It was only a few minutes before nine in the evening when he realized he was walking back down Seminole Boulevard toward his apartment. Traffic hummed this way and that; several pedestrians were seen, on their merry way to wherever; a plane flew silently overhead below an endless sea of stars. Stores and restaurants were lit up and full of normalcy.

Sharsted smiled.

And unless Raguel's a bigtime liar, I've still got thirteen more years to live, and after that I die and go to Purgatory, and whatever I gotta do to get out of Purgatory... He shrugged. *I'll do. Pray a lot, I guess. Praise God and all that...*

Then he thought, *Bonus!* when he errantly reached into his pocket and found it fat with the two bands of hundred-dollar bills he'd been granted at the drug apartment. *Yeah! It's a beautiful day in the neighborhood!*

Sharsted then—

KUR-CLUNK!

—got run over in the road by a red Mitsubishi Eclipse and a tattooed young woman in an

UberEats hat.

He'd been proceeding happily through the walk-light at the very same crosswalk where the man in the wheelchair had been hit earlier. Like something out of a tawdry Hollywood thriller, he felt himself be drawn under the car's front bumper in slow-motion, gradually being fed beneath the vehicle's wheels, hearing his bones crunch, and watching the underside of the vehicle pass over his astonished gaze.

The rear tires kicked him out onto the street in the car's wake. Broken-boned and waylaid, his cheek was pressed against asphalt and he was able to watch the Eclipse accelerate and make a quick right at the next turn, squealing wheels.

A raging ripoff? An example of unmitigated deceit?

No.

Sharsted would awake some days later, in a comfortable hospital bed; therefore, he hadn't been lied to at all.

However, he was paralyzed from the neck down, unable even to speak, and it was in this state that he would remain until his death on the Ides of March at the age of seventy-nine, immediately after which he would find himself in the pitch-black darkness of Purgatory, where he would likely spend the next couple of thousand years listening to distant chatter and moans, floating about with no sense of up, down, right, or left, and cringing every time a pair of dry dusty hands emerged to paw at his face without relent.

There would be many such pairs of hands, and they would visit him regularly.

NIPPING THEM IN THE BUD

ABOUT THE AUTHOR

Edward Lee is an American novelist specializing in the field of horror, and has authored over 50 books. Lee is particularly known for over-the-top occult concepts and an accelerated treatment of erotic and/or morbid sexual imagery and visceral violence.

www.ingramcontent.com/pod-product-compliance
Lightning Source LLC
Chambersburg PA
CBHW072011170626
46813CB00005B/2108